PRAISE FOR THE NOVELS OF KIMBERLA LAWSON ROBY

The Reverend's Wife

"Engrossing...The writing is cinematic and the juicy plot moves quickly...Roby has a talent for underscoring the universal challenges of people of faith."   —*Publishers Weekly*

"Roby writes with high-octane levels of emotion. She pushes her characters hard, spotlighting their flaws, showcasing their weaknesses, drawing in the readers to be more than bystanders."
     —*USA Today*'s Happy Ever After blog

"[Roby] knows how to give readers what they want."   —*Essence*

"4 stars! There's nothing like a healthy dose of drama to keep readers on their toes. Underneath the deception, gossip, and bad decisions lies a storyline that any reader will be able to relate to. The author paints an interesting story with an accurate view of what goes on within the family behind the pulpit."
     —*RT Book Reviews*

"Definitely a page-turner with new and crazy characters. I love how Roby gives each of the Blacks an opportunity for their own story...If you are in love with these characters, you will love this book. And even if you have never read a book in this series, you will enjoy this one."   —APOOOBooks.com

"5 stars! The Blacks are back and better than ever... *The Reverend's Wife* has a storyline that flows effortlessly and the characters pop with so much life and realism, you can't help but become involved... Roby has done it again, and it's even better than the last time!... a guaranteed page-turner with enough drama and surprises to keep you hooked till the jaw-dropping ending."   —AAMBookClub.com

Secret Obsession

"Roby is the queen of redemption! She has a knack for taking characters that readers love to hate and turning them into ones everyone will cheer for. This one's definitely a page-turner!"
                                                                —*RT Book Reviews*

"Filled with unexpected twists and turns... a dramatic, engaging, and entertaining piece of work."   —*Prominence Magazine*

"The lengths Paige goes to... sure keep the pages turning... Fans of Roby's Curtis Black novels will find this one true to form."   —*Booklist*

"An exciting page-turner!"   —*Upscale*

"[A] juicy read!"   —*Essence*

"*New York Times* bestselling author Kimberla Lawson Roby has a knack for writing suspenseful, page-turning stories, and her latest novel, *Secret Obsession*, is no different... A must-read for fiction thriller fans."   —TheRoot.com

"The kind of novel I wish more authors would write...addictive."   —ChickLitReviewsandNews.com

Love, Honor, and Betray

"For those thousands of fans, who can't get enough of the 'good' reverend and his wives, this is a book that should not be missed."
                                                                    —Philly.com

"Lively, action packed, and full of sassy sensuality, Roby once again has created a story that grabs the reader's attention and holds it until the very end."   —*Las Vegas Review-Journal*

"An entertaining read...remains true to Roby's style of creatively telling a story."   —*New York Amsterdam News*

"Like her previous fiction, *Love, Honor, and Betray* provides an unflinching examination of the human condition while keeping the reader engaged and entertained at the same time."
                                                                    —Examiner.com

"Much of Kimberla Lawson Roby's bestselling success is due to her irresistibly complex character Rev. Curtis Black. In *Love, Honor, and Betray*, her eighth [book] about the self-justifying, greedy, womanizing minister, she tackles one of the most challenging situations facing the explosion of blended families today."   —*Heart & Soul*

"Full of drama and splashed with plenty of suspense and love triangles."   —*Upscale*

The Perfect Marriage

Also by Kimberla Lawson Roby

THE REVEREND CURTIS BLACK SERIES

A House Divided
The Reverend's Wife
Love, Honor, and Betray
Be Careful What You Pray For
The Best of Everything
Sin No More
Love & Lies
The Best-Kept Secret
Too Much of a Good Thing
Casting the First Stone

STAND-ALONE TITLES

The Perfect Marriage
Secret Obsession
A Deep Dark Secret
One in a Million
Changing Faces
A Taste of Reality
It's a Thin Line
Here & Now
Behind Closed Doors

The Perfect Marriage

KIMBERLA LAWSON ROBY

GRAND CENTRAL
PUBLISHING

NEW YORK   BOSTON

Grand Central Publishing
Hachette Book Group
237 Park Avenue
New York, NY 10017

www.HachetteBookGroup.com

Printed in the United States of America

RRD-C

First trade edition: September 2013
10 9 8 7 6 5 4 3 2 1

Grand Central Publishing is a division of Hachette Book Group, Inc. The Grand Central Publishing name and logo is a trademark of Hachette Book Group, Inc.

The Hachette Speakers Bureau provides a wide range of authors for speaking events. To find out more, go to www.hachettespeakersbureau.com or call (866) 376-6591.

The publisher is not responsible for websites (or their content) that are not owned by the publisher.

The Library of Congress has cataloged the hardcover edition as follows:
Roby, Kimberla Lawson.
The perfect marriage / Kimberla Lawson Roby. -- 1st ed.
p. cm.
ISBN 978-0-446-57250-7 (regular edition) -- ISBN 978-1-4555-2246-0 (large print edition) 1. Family secrets--Fiction. 2. African American families--Fiction. 3. Marriage--Fiction. 4. Domestic fiction. I. Title.
PS3568.O3189P47 2013
813'.54--dc23

2012016128

ISBN 978-0-446-57249-1 (pbk.)

For my uncle—Luther Tennin
(August 22, 1932–April 3, 2012)
I miss you dearly and will love you always.

Acknowledgments

Many, many thanks to God for so much grace, mercy, and Your abundant blessings; to my wonderful husband, Will, for more love and support than any wife could ever ask for—I love you from the bottom of my heart and soul; to my brothers, Willie Jr. and Michael, for all the wonderful childhood memories and adult memories and for giving me nieces and nephews that I love like my own children—I love you both so very much; to my step-son and daughter-in-law, Trenod and Tasha, and your children—I love you dearly; to the rest of my loving family—I love you all: Tennins, Ballards, Lawsons, Stapletons, Youngs, Beasleys, Haleys, Romes, Greens, Robys, Garys, Shannons, Normans, and everyone else I'm blessed to be related to! To my first cousin and fellow author, Patricia, for all the fun childhood memories and for those we are still creating decades later and to my girls of girls, Kelli, Lori, and Janell, for absolutely everything—I love all four of you so very much; to my spiritual mother, Dr. Betty Price, whom I love dearly; to my publishing attorney, Ken Norwick, for such great representation; to the best publisher in the whole wide world, Grand Central Publishing: Jamie Raab, Beth de Guzman, Selina McLemore, Linda Duggins, Elizabeth Connor, Dorothea Halliday, the entire sales and marketing teams, and everyone else at GCP! To the best freelance team ever, Connie Dettman, Shandra Hill Smith, Luke LeFevre, and Pam Walker-Williams—thank you all for everything! To every bookseller who sells my work, every newspaper, radio station, TV station, and online website or blog that promotes my work, and to every book club that continually chooses my work as your monthly selection—thanks a million.

Finally, to the folks who go out of their way to make my writing career possible—**my wonderfully kind and supportive readers**. I love you with everything in me, and I am forever grateful to **ALL** of you.

Much love and God bless you always,

Kimberla Lawson Roby

E-Mail: kim@kimroby.com
Facebook: www.facebook.com/kimberlalawsonroby
Twitter: www.twitter.com/KimberlaLRoby

The Perfect Marriage

Prologue

"Hi, I'm Jackson," the fifty-something man dressed in a pair of work overalls said.

"Hi, Jackson." Twenty-two men and women of various ethnic backgrounds spoke back to him in unison. They sat around three banquet-length tables that were pushed together as one, and Denise wanted to hightail it out of there as fast as she could. For nearly an hour, she and her husband, Derrek, both of them dressed in professional business suits, had listened to one recovering drug addict after another, sharing multiple horror stories; yet Denise still couldn't understand why they were there—why they were humiliating themselves in such a very shameful way. It was true that during the wee hours of the morning, Derrek had awakened from a torturous nightmare and had decided that they both needed serious help, but Denise honestly couldn't have disagreed with him more. She couldn't fathom any of his thinking because the truth of the matter was, she and Derrek weren't the least bit addicted to anything. She did take Vicodin nightly for relaxation purposes, what with all the major stress she endured as director of nursing for one of the Chicago area's largest nursing homes, but finding various ways to relax was normal for just about anyone she could think of. Then, as far as Derrek was concerned, about a year ago he'd begun snorting a little cocaine socially with a couple of his close colleagues, but that was it. Of course, he hadn't actually planned on telling Denise about his newfound indulgence but when she'd accidentally discovered a small plastic baggie in his blazer pocket of all places, filled with some white powdery substance, she'd confronted him. He'd apologized for hiding things from her, and while she hadn't necessarily liked the idea of him using an illegal drug, she also couldn't deny that she'd always been curious about it herself. Her parents had raised her to be a "good girl," and when she'd become a teenager, they'd kept her away from "bad girl" sorts of things, such as late-night parties and the kind of friends who could do whatever they wanted when they wanted to. Her father had also forbade her to be friends with any child—even her own cousins—who didn't live in a "suitable" neighborhood and didn't attend private school. He'd made it very clear that she wasn't to consort with "riffraff" of any kind unless their parents were of a certain class.

In the end, her parents had basically guarded her day and night, told her that she didn't need many friends anyway, and had insisted she should focus mainly on being the best student possible. They'd also encouraged her to read her Bible daily and had kept her frequently involved in church activities. This, of course, had been fine, though, because it was Denise's upbringing that had stopped her from doing anything that wasn't good for her, specifically during her college years. She hadn't even dated all that much back then and had primarily concentrated on her studies and potentially bright future in nursing. She'd learned to do exactly as her father had expected, and she'd gone very far in life because of it.

Still, for some reason, she'd always wondered what it would be like to smoke marijuana, or even snort a little cocaine, for that matter, simply because she'd never done anything irrational.

Maybe her strong interest in trying drugs stemmed from how strict her parents had been and the fact that everything had been so off-limits. Because no matter how much education she'd gotten or how often she'd gone to church, she'd never been able to shed this relentless need to do something out of the ordinary— something wild even. She'd known it was crazy and lowly of her to even consider such things, which was the reason she'd never shared these feelings with another living soul, but her curiosity was what it was and she couldn't help it—so much so that when the opportunity had presented itself, she'd taken it. She'd debated back and forth and then back and forth again, but three months ago when she'd found herself home alone taking a much needed day off from work, she'd pulled out Derrek's stash from the tan metal box he kept it in. Even then, as she'd held it in her hand, she'd debated a while longer but then she had finally poured a tiny line of cocaine onto one of her hand mirrors and snorted it with a straw she'd gotten from the kitchen. At first, she'd wondered how long it would take before she felt anything, but in a couple of minutes, she'd gotten her first buzz. She remembered, too, how she'd never felt more energized or stress-free in her life.

So over these last three months, she and Derrek sometimes— well every night that is—did a line or two in their bedroom. They only did it, though, as a way to unwind, so why not? Especially since not only was her job extremely demanding and filled with loads of responsibility, Derrek's position as director of finance at Covington Park Memorial Hospital was just as taxing. They both worked long hours, they did all they could trying to be the best parents they could be to their twelve-year-old daughter, Mackenzie, and at the end of every given workday a bit of cocaine always made them feel better. It took the edge off in more ways than one, but again, they weren't hooked and had not a thing to worry about.

But here the two of them were, front and center, sitting at some humdrum Narcotics Anonymous meeting among people who truly *were* addicts—folks who didn't appear to have ever lived the kind of decent life she and Derrek had worked so hard to establish. As Denise scanned the entire group one by one, she did feel sorry for these poor people, but she also couldn't help noticing that she and Derrek had nothing in common with them. Many had talked about their days of being homeless, some had mentioned not graduating from high school, and others had talked about the horrible neighborhoods they'd grown up in. Just about every single story had depressed Denise, and she wanted to leave.

So much for wishful thinking, though, because as soon as Jackson finished sharing about his last few days, Derrek spoke next.

"Hi, I'm Derrek."

"Hi, Derrek," everyone said, some smiling and some with quiet stares.

"Well, I'm not sure where to begin exactly, so I guess I'll just say that I'm very glad to be here. My wife and I," he said, looking at Denise, "have never attended any kind of meetings for addiction before, but one thing I'll never forget are the stories my grandfather told me for years about his days as an alcoholic. He would tell me how it was the worst time in his life and that had it not been for God and Alcoholics Anonymous, he would have likely been a dead man in his thirties. Before he died, he'd been sober for almost forty years, but even then, he still attended one or two meetings every week."

Many of the people around the table nodded, more of them smiling than before, and Denise hoped Derrek wasn't going to share any more of their personal business. She wondered why he couldn't handle this *so-called* drug problem in private. Some time ago, Derrek had gotten a little carried away with playing the Illinois State Lottery, but when he'd realized enough was enough, he'd prayed about it and stopped on his own. He hadn't needed any twelve-step program back then, so for the life of her, she couldn't understand why this new issue was different.

Now, instead of *hoping* he wouldn't say anything else, she wanted to *beg* him not to.

But sadly, he did.

"The real reason I wanted my wife and I to come tonight, though, is because I had this horrifying dream that scared me to death. It was very vivid and when it was all said and done, my wife and I had ended up just like my parents: strung out on drugs and living on the street. We were homeless and destitute."

Everyone stared at Derrek, attentively and compassionately, and Denise could tell their hearts went out to him—and her, too, for that matter. The only thing was, she and Derrek *didn't* have a problem, and she wished he'd stop blowing everything out of proportion and being so dramatic.

"Anyway, I won't take up a lot of your time tonight, but again, I'm very glad to be here and thank you for having us."

"Thanks, Derrek. Keep coming back." Everyone spoke together in an almost chantlike fashion.

Derrek nodded. "I will."

Denise wanted to scream.

Chapter 1

Two Months Later

Denise smoothed the back of her husband's head, admiring how handsome he still was, and gazed at their beautiful daughter. She honestly couldn't have been happier. They were all sitting in the family room, she and Derrek on the soft, plush, burnt-orange leather sofa and Mackenzie in one of the matching oversize chairs. Mackenzie's long, slender legs were propped up on one of the ottomans as she sipped strawberry soda from an ice-filled glass. Tonight was pizza night and while Denise hadn't eaten any, Mackenzie and her father had devoured as much as they could. They were also in the midst of watching *The Color Purple* for the umpteenth time and were enjoying every minute of it.

But as Denise glanced over at Derrek again, she thought about how blessed they truly were. They'd been married for fifteen wonderful years, she still loved him more than ever, and he clearly felt the same about her. She knew there was no such thing as a perfect marriage, but if there had been, her marriage to Derrek would certainly have to qualify; partly because they undoubtedly had the love of a lifetime and partly because no disagreement or problem had ever come between them. Then, if that wasn't enough, God had blessed them with the best daughter. She was kind and smart, she loved everyone she came in contact with, and she never got into trouble. She also had a knack for helping any of her schoolmates who were a lot less fortunate than her whenever they were in need of something. She'd been gifted with an old soul for sure, and she was the kind of child any parent could be proud of.

Then, in addition to their marriage and daughter, God had given them both successful careers. They'd each graduated from top schools, she from Johns Hopkins University with a bachelor's degree in nursing and then a master's in nursing from the University of Illinois at Chicago, and Derrek from Northwestern with a bachelor's in business and then an MBA from the same grad school as her. Denise had gone to college on a partial academic scholarship, but it also hadn't been a problem for her parents to cover the balance of her tuition since her father had been a top criminal defense attorney in downtown Chicago for years. Derrek, on the other hand, hadn't come from a well-to-do family and had been forced to struggle and work his way through school. He'd also had to utilize as many grants and student loans as had been available to him. As a matter of fact, because Derrek's parents had gotten so caught up with drugs, it had been his maternal grandparents who had raised him and his twin brother, Dixon. Neither of his grandparents had earned huge salaries, but they'd still given their two grandsons a good home and had done the best they could with them.

When Denise heard Shug Avery saying, "I's married now," she gazed at the large flat-screen television and thought about her own wedding. The ceremony had been amazing, and she still remembered every detail like it was yesterday. Eight bridesmaids, eight groomsmen, two maids of honor, two best men, three gorgeous little flower girls, the most handsome little ring bearer, and nearly five hundred guests. It had all been a dream come true for both Denise and Derrek, and their family members had been just as happy. In fact, life had been good since the very first day they'd met, which had sort of happened by accident. Right after completing her nursing program, Denise had immediately gotten hired by Covington Park Memorial, and as it had turned out, Derrek had started working for the hospital's finance department the same week. But the reason she'd always felt their meeting had been by accident was because she'd received employment offers from two other hospitals in the Chicago area, and it hadn't been until a couple of days before her scheduled hire date that she'd decided against one of them and had checked to see if the offer was still on the table from Covington. She'd changed her mind at the last minute for no particular reason, although her mom always insisted that there were no such things as accidents or coincidences, only meant-to-be situations. Her mom believed that everything truly did happen for a reason.

Derrek laughed at one of the funnier scenes in the movie and grabbed Denise's hand. The romance between them was still very much alive, and she couldn't be more grateful. The only thing was, however, suddenly, she felt somewhat out of sorts and a bit uneasy. She knew why, though: she'd had another long, hectic day at work, and she needed something to calm her nerves. Nothing major but just a little something to help her through the rest of the evening and prepare her for a restful night of sleep. But just as she started to get up, Mackenzie said, "Oh Mom and Dad, I forgot to tell you. Alexis's parents are leaving two days earlier than we are for their Christmas trip, so is it okay for her to stay here with us?"

"Of course," Denise said. "She's traveling with us for the holidays, anyway."

"I told her you wouldn't mind, but she still wanted me to ask. I think her mom is going to call you."

"It's no problem at all."

"Gosh, only three more months," Mackenzie said, beaming. "Jamaica is gonna be so much fun, and I'm so glad Alexis is going. We're gonna have an even better time than we had on the cruise last year."

"I'm excited, too," Denise said just before Mackenzie's phone rang.

Derrek pressed the Pause button on the DVR, and Mackenzie checked her Caller ID screen.

"This is Alexis now. I'll call her back, though, when the movie goes off."

"You sure?" he asked.

"Uh-huh."

Derrek pressed the Play button, and Denise scooted toward the edge of the sofa. "I need to review a couple of care plan files for tomorrow, but I'll be back down in a half hour or so."

Mackenzie looked at her mother. "But Mom, you're gonna miss the rest of the movie."

"Well, maybe not all of it. I'll try to finish up as soon as I can."

Mackenzie didn't say anything else and turned back toward the television. Derrek did the same, and Denise strolled through the hallway and up the carpeted winding staircase. They'd only lived in this particular house for five years, but it was their dream home. They'd owned two houses prior to this, first their starter home, which had been fifteen hundred square feet, then their second, which was nearly double that size, and now this one, which was right at five thousand. There were three finished levels that included four bedrooms, a theater room, an exercise room, and three fireplaces. They'd built it brand new, so not only was this their third home, it was their last. This was the house they would retire in and the one they would eventually sell many years from now when they were too old and too tired to worry about normal upkeep. They would then happily and readily scale down to a nice little condo.

Denise stepped inside her bedroom, closed the door and hurried over to her handbag. She'd gone all day without taking anything, but now her stress level was getting the best of her. So, she unzipped the middle compartment, pulled out an unlabeled bottle and opened it. She tapped it with her left forefinger until one large, white, oblong pill fell into her hand. Then, she went into the bathroom and turned on the faucet. She wasn't too keen on drinking from the tap, mainly because she was so used to drinking bottled water, but she knew tap would have to do because she didn't want to traipse all the way back downstairs to the kitchen and take a chance on Derrek seeing her and questioning what she was doing.

She ran the water for sixty seconds or so, waiting for it to cool down, and then she lifted a decorative cup from the top of the vanity. When it was half full, she tossed the Vicodin into her mouth, gulped down some water and swallowed. She immediately drank the rest of it, went back into the bedroom and sat in one of the high-back chairs in the sitting area. Then she waited. She did this because she knew her body would be relaxed in no time. She'd been pretty hungry when she'd first gotten home, but the reason she hadn't eaten pizza with Derrek and Mackenzie was because a few months ago she'd learned that when she took Vicodin on an empty stomach the euphoria was much more intense and it gave her a warm feeling. It also only took thirty minutes or less to take full effect, and this was the reason she'd had no choice but to lie to her daughter about having to go upstairs to work. She hated being dishonest, but she'd needed an excuse to get away for at least forty-five minutes to an hour so she could enjoy the way the Vicodin made her feel. She would also take another before going to bed. Not because she needed to, but because she wanted to. She knew Derrek wouldn't agree and wouldn't understand, but no matter what he said, she saw nothing inappropriate about feeling good. She also knew he'd be livid if he somehow discovered that she hadn't fully given up cocaine, either, or that she'd secretly found her own dealer to buy from. Derrek was still dead set on going to those Narcotics Anonymous meetings every now and then, meaning he hadn't done any cocaine since that first gathering he'd dragged her along to, but Denise hadn't gone back. She also knew Derrek wouldn't be happy if he found out she now took Vicodin on a pretty regular basis—even though the pain in her hip, a result of her falling on a sheet of ice, had vanished months ago. He'd be terribly disappointed if he ever learned that her orthopedic specialist hadn't written her a prescription for Vicodin ever since and he would certainly hit the roof if he somehow discovered that she now got her pills any way she could: at first from doctor friends, who hadn't seemed to mind writing her a prescription, but when they'd eventually stopped taking her calls, she'd begun buying them from the same guy who sold her cocaine. Actually, it was a good thing she was the one who handled their family finances because it was for this reason that Derrek hadn't noticed the extra money she was spending.

But no matter how Denise looked at things, she saw nothing wrong with any of what she was doing. Not when she clearly had total control and wasn't addicted to anything. Still, she would keep her Vicodin and cocaine moments to herself. She decided her silence was best for everyone involved.

Chapter 2

Derrek was repositioning his tie in front of the dresser mirror, making sure it wasn't crooked, when the home phone rang. It was pretty early on a Friday morning for anyone to be calling, but when he stepped closer to the phone on the nightstand and saw that it was his brother, Dixon, he rolled his eyes and ignored it. He was glad that even though a lot of time had passed, Dixon still had the same cell number because had he changed it, Derrek might have thought someone else was calling and he could have made the mistake of answering.

"Who's that?" Denise asked.

"Nobody."

Denise shook her head, slipped on one of her hoop earrings and snapped it closed. "So honey, exactly how long are you planning to go without speaking to your brother? It's been at least three years now."

"Yeah, and I still don't have a thing to say to him."

Just thinking about the way Dixon had treated him was enough to piss Derrek off. Derrek had done everything for his brother—his twin brother at that—but all Dixon had done was lie, tell more lies, and use Derrek every chance he got. He was outrageously selfish and while Derrek had allowed Dixon to borrow money multiple times, promise to pay it back, and never make good on it, the stunt he'd pulled three years ago had been too much. For years, Derrek had loaned Dixon two hundred here and five hundred there, but with this last occurrence, Dixon had called him up claiming he'd been laid off from his job and that he needed five thousand dollars to cover his bills: mortgage, car note, utilities, and a few medical expenses. Derrek had known it was a lot of money to be loaning anyone, even his own brother, but after he and Denise had discussed it and Dixon had sworn he would pay them back just as soon as he borrowed money from his retirement account, Derrek had gone to the bank and gotten a cashier's check. Dixon had thanked him profusely and promised again that he would repay the money in a couple of weeks or so. Sadly, a couple of weeks had come and gone and by the time a full month had passed, Derrek had learned from a mutual friend that Dixon had taken his girlfriend on a ten-day trip to Paris. Derrek hadn't wanted to believe his own flesh and blood would deceive him this way, but sure enough when he'd called Dixon and questioned him about the money, Dixon had stuttered between words but then flat out told Derrek, "I don't have it." Then, when Derrek had asked him about the trip, Dixon had said, "Look, man...okay, yeah, it's true. I took my girl on a nice vacation just like you do with Denise every year. So why don't you stop badgering me about that funky little five thousand dollars? It's not like you need it right back anyhow." Derrek remembered how he'd almost cracked up laughing at his brother because surely he couldn't have been serious. Surely he hadn't meant a word he'd just said and had only been joking. But after thirty seconds of total silence, Derrek quickly realized his brother *had* meant every word he'd said, and Derrek hadn't spoken to Dixon ever since.

"Honey, are you listening to me?" Derrek heard Denise saying.

"I'm sorry, baby, I guess I was somewhere else."

Denise ran a brush through her bouncy, black, shoulder-length hair and moved closer to him. "You were thinking about your brother, weren't you?"

"Yeah, but not anymore."

"Honey, I really wish you would talk to Dixon. Listen to what he has to say and then just forgive him. Life is way too short for this."

"Dixon should have thought about that three years ago."

Denise set the brush on the dresser and held Derrek's hands. "I understand how you feel, but baby he made a mistake. And it was a long time ago."

Derrek gazed at her with sad eyes. "I appreciate what you're trying to do, but as far as I'm concerned, I don't even have a brother."

Denise walked back over to the bed and placed a few items in her purse. Derrek could tell she wasn't happy with his response, but he couldn't help the way he felt. A part of him wished he could let bygones be bygones because sometimes he truly missed his brother, but for some reason he just couldn't. Not this time. Not when his brother had totally disrespected him and acted as though what he'd done was no big deal. Not when his brother had hurt him to the core, knowing full well that the two of them had already suffered more than enough during childhood. In fact, his mother and father had left both of them with such painful memories, Derrek still hadn't forgiven them, either. How could he? How could anyone forgive a mother and a father who could so easily choose drugs over their own children? Leave two little eight-year-old boys home alone for days without food or clean clothing? How could Derrek forgive any adult who could be so awful to any human being?

That had been almost thirty years ago, but sometimes the mere thought of his parents and what they'd done to him and

Dixon brought Derrek to tears. After all this time, he still hadn't gotten completely over his childhood and wondered if he ever would.

There was something great that had resulted from it all, though: his grandparents. They'd both passed away a few years back, but he thanked God for them because had they not brought him and Dixon to come live with them, he wasn't sure how their lives might have turned out. His childhood woes were also the reason he'd sworn he'd never be anything like his parents—the reason he loved, honored, and cherished his gorgeous wife, the reason having a close relationship with his daughter was so important. It was also because of his parents that he'd vowed to never do drugs under any circumstances. To his great disappointment, though, he'd resorted to using cocaine. He hadn't planned on doing it, but one day he'd gone to a colleague's home to watch a football game and the next thing he'd known, one of the guys had passed him a line, and he'd taken a hit. It had been the stupidest thing in the world for him to do, but it also hadn't taken him long to realize how much he liked it. He'd loved how free it made him feel and how the emotional stress he'd struggled with since that morning hadn't mattered to him for the rest of the evening. To this day, he still hadn't told Denise what had triggered his decision to try cocaine for the first time because he hadn't wanted to upset her—and he never would tell her—but earlier that day he'd been told he might have cancer. His doctor had run a couple of scans on what had seemed like some sort of small, malignant tumor in his groin area, but once the growth had been removed and a biopsy had been performed, Derrek had learned it was benign. He hadn't been told the final results, though, until a couple of days after his initial scare and by then, Derrek had snorted cocaine three evenings straight. He hadn't wanted to stop, and for the rest of the week, he'd simply told Denise that he'd been working late. Ironically, she actually *had* been working longer hours than usual, so with her being much too tired for sex for a period of days, she'd never even noticed his scar.

Thankfully, though, that terrifying dream he'd had two months ago had made him think long and hard, and he was glad he'd come to his senses—glad he'd realized that he and Denise had begun loving cocaine just a bit too much and that he'd suggested they go to a Narcotics Anonymous meeting. No, they hadn't lost their jobs and cleaned out their savings accounts, nor were they living on the street, but just knowing that he and Denise had begun snorting lines together every evening had made him think. It was true that maybe his insisting that they attend a meeting centered on a twelve-step program was a bit over the top, but nonetheless, it had stopped them both from getting high and he was happy about that.

After Derek slipped on his shoes and tied them, he grabbed his blazer. Denise slid on her watch, snapped the clasp shut, and they headed downstairs. Mackenzie was already parked at the granite-topped island eating a bowl of cereal and reading one of her textbooks, and Denise went over to the coffeepot. For years she'd been adding fresh coffee grounds to the filter each night before going to bed, so all she did now was press the Start button.

"Sweetie, you have debate practice after school today, right?" Denise asked Mackenzie, because on those days, Mackenzie couldn't take the bus home or carpool with her friends who had stay-at-home moms. Either Derek or Denise had to pick her up.

"Yep. Oh and we're staying an extra two hours tonight. Mr. Braxton says we need to put in a little more time this week, so we'll be ready for the competition next Thursday."

"So is the topic still about K–12 students in the state of Illinois and whether they should attend school year round?"

"Yep. And while I don't necessarily think it would be good for any of us to go without a summer break, I'm sort of glad our team will be showing the benefits of it. There's so much information out there to support that particular aspect of the argument."

Denise smiled. "I'm so glad you joined the debate team. I loved being on debate when I was in school because we learned so much about controversial topics."

Derrek placed two slices of bread in the toaster. "I loved being on the team, too, when I was your age. I was also on the high school team all four years," he said, looking over at the ringing phone. It was Dixon again, and Derrek pretended not to hear it.

Mackenzie watched him move to the other side of the kitchen. "Daddy, is that Uncle Dixon calling?"

"Unfortunately, it is, sweetie."

"Well, Daddy, why won't you talk to him? And why can't I see him anymore?"

"I'm sorry things aren't good between my brother and me, but you'll understand when you're older. Plus, if your uncle really wanted to talk to us or even apologize, he'd leave a message."

Mackenzie lowered her eyes. "Maybe he's afraid to."

Derrek didn't say anything.

Still she continued, "Daddy, I think you're wrong to treat Uncle Dixon like this because by now, I'm sure even God has forgiven him for whatever he did."

Denise finally chimed in, and Derrek was surprised she hadn't done so before now. "Sweetie, you're right," she said. "God forgives us for everything. All we have to do is ask Him."

Two against one. Derrek knew there was no way to win this conversation, so he flipped the television on and turned it to CNN. He watched Soledad O'Brien, Roland Martin, David Gergen, and two other popular political analysts for a few minutes, but once the coffee was ready, he drank a cup, ate his toast, and grabbed his briefcase. But the phone rang again.

Denise walked over to it. "Baby, why don't you at least see what your brother wants? He's made a lot of calls over the last few days. For at least a week now."

Derrek did something that was rare for him: he blatantly ignored his wife's comment. "Mackenzie, if you're ready, we'd better get going. Unless you want to take the bus." He always teased his daughter every chance he got about getting rides versus taking the bus, but today he did it as a way to change the subject.

Denise folded her arms, though, clearly aware of what he was up to.

"I'm sorry," he said, walking over and kissing her on the lips.

"I just wish you'd rethink your position on this."

"I love you," he said. "And I'll see you later."

Derrek kissed her again and walked out to the garage. He wished he could feel differently but if his brother didn't stop calling, Derrek would contact the phone company and have his number blocked. He would do whatever he had to do to get rid of him.

Chapter 3

Denise sifted through several documents, searching for a file containing résumés from potential new hires, hoping she'd be able to fill a few RN openings as soon as possible. They were noticeably understaffed, thanks to another suburban nursing home offering RNs much higher signing bonuses and hourly pay, and Denise needed to find qualified candidates. The new pay scale and signing amounts at the other facility had come out of nowhere, and four of her best nurses had quickly given their notices. They'd jumped ship, and while Denise hadn't blamed them, she didn't like the strain it had left on the remaining staff members, and, of course, her. Things were busy as ever, and sometimes whole workdays vanished so frantically she never even knew where they went. This was the reason, too, that she'd discussed higher salaries and new employment incentives with her boss, Mr. Hunter, because they could never experience this kind of situation again.

Denise read through the first two résumés in the pile but looked up when someone knocked at her door.

"Come in."

Pamela, her second-floor nursing supervisor, entered. She stroked her blond hair away from her face, and Denise could tell she was frustrated.

"I'm sorry to bother you, Denise, but Agatha Bowman is demanding to see 'the person who runs this place.'"

"Lord, the woman has only been here two days, yet she's had more complaints than every resident combined. So now what?"

"Who knows? I tried asking her, but all she did was purse her lips and look out the window."

"Okayyy," Denise sang. "Let's go see what Miss Agatha wants."

Denise and Pamela left the office and walked a few steps toward the elevator. When the door opened, they stepped on and rode one floor up. Agatha's room was only a few doors down the hallway, so it didn't take long to get there. When they walked in, Agatha, a refined and very wealthy eighty-one-year-old, frowned. She sat in her bed propped against three pillows.

"Are you the person in charge?"

"For the most part. I'm the director of nursing. We met last week, remember?"

"I remember perfectly, but since I specifically asked to see the person who runs this place, I figured maybe you'd been promoted. Maybe you were the new head honcho." Her tone was sarcastic, and Denise knew this conversation wasn't going to be pretty.

"Mr. Hunter wasn't available, so I asked Denise to come," Pamela added.

Agatha looked away from them. "Well, I'll just wait until he *is* available."

Denise wondered why the woman was being so difficult when all she and Pamela were trying to do was help her.

"Maybe if you can tell me what the problem is I can relay it to Mr. Hunter. Then he can come see you when he's free."

Agatha folded her arms but still wouldn't look at them. "Like I said... I'll just wait."

"Are you sure there's nothing I can do for you in the mean-time?"

"Positive."

Denise and Pamela looked at each other and started to leave.

"Oh and just so you know," Agatha told them. "If I don't see Mr. Hunter before the day is out, I'm contacting the proper authorities."

Denise didn't bother commenting, but a complaint of any kind to the state of Illinois, legitimate or otherwise, was never good and it was the last thing they needed. Not to mention, Agatha Bowman was extremely well off and would certainly do exactly what she promised. There was no question about it, so Denise walked straight over to the nurses' station and dialed Mr. Hunter. His assistant answered immediately.

"Hi, Carla, it's Denise."

"How are you?"

"I've been better. But hey, is Mr. Hunter still unavailable?"

"Actually, he was on a conference call but he just hung up. I'll transfer you."

"Thanks." Denise waited a few seconds until her boss picked up.

"Hi, Denise."

"I'm really sorry to bother you, but we have a situation. Agatha Bowman isn't happy, and she refuses to talk to anyone except you."

"No problem. I'll be right there."

"I really appreciate it."

In the meantime, Denise conversed with a couple of certified nursing assistants about their upcoming weekend off and soon Mr. Hunter approached the desk. Denise apologized again, and the two of them headed down the hallway and into Agatha's room.

Mr. Hunter moved closer to her bed. "Well, good morning, Agatha."

"It would be if people did their jobs."

"What seems to be the problem?"

Agatha pointed toward the floor on the other side of her bed.

Mr. Hunter strolled over to the window, bent down, and picked up a large bath towel. "This?"

"Yes!"

If Denise hadn't seen this charade with her own eyes, she never would have believed it. All this commotion and the need to see the head honcho because of a towel?

"My apologies to you," Mr. Hunter said. "Our staff members really should be more careful, and I'll make sure this doesn't happen again."

"I hope you do because at five thousand dollars a month, I won't tolerate this kind of incompetence. Nor will my son if I tell him about it."

"You have my word. And is there anything else I can do for you?"

"No, that'll be all."

"Also," Mr. Hunter added, "Denise here is the best director I've had. So if you have any more concerns, please let us know. Either one of us will be happy to help you."

Agatha slipped on a pair of reading glasses and peered over the top of them. "It's always been my experience that the only way to guarantee speedy results is by going straight to the top."

Denise could tell Agatha was trying Mr. Hunter's patience but all he said was, "We're very sorry for the dirty towel being on your floor."

"Apology accepted, now if you don't mind, I'd like to do some reading."

This woman was a piece of work, and as soon as they stepped

outside of her room, Mr. Hunter dropped the towel in a bin and walked over to the instant sanitizer dispenser. He squirted a portion into his hands and vigorously rubbed them together. As they walked toward the elevator, though, he finally said, "Why is it always the wealthy ones who give us such a hard time? I mean, it's not all wealthy patients who act this way, but usually when we get someone complaining about nothing, they're usually people who have the kind of money Agatha does."

"I don't know, but you're definitely right. Hopefully, she'll settle down as time goes on."

"We'll see."

They waited for the elevator, but before the doors could open, one of the new LPNs walked up to them. Tammy was twenty-two, petite, and as cute as could be.

"Denise, Pamela wanted me to try to catch you before you went back to your office. Lula Mitchell's vitals aren't very good, and her breathing seems a bit irregular."

"Is Pamela with her now?"

"Yes."

Denise looked at Mr. Hunter. "Duty calls."

"As always. See ya."

Denise and Tammy strolled around the corner and into Lula's room. Pamela was checking her blood pressure again.

"How is it?" Denise asked.

"Ninety over fifty."

Denise walked over to the bed and took Lula's hand. Lula was such a sweetheart, and she was one of Denise's favorite people. "So how are you feeling, Lula?"

Lula tried smiling as best she could, but her voice was weak. "I'm okay."

"Are you having trouble breathing?"

"A little."

"I think we should have her transported over to the hospital. Just to check her out."

"I'll call for an ambulance and then call her doctor," Pamela said. "And Tammy, why don't you ask one of the CNAs to come help get Lula dressed."

"Will do."

Denise patted Lula's hand. "You're going to be fine, okay? You'll be back here in no time."

"Thank you, Denise. You all take such good care of me, and I really appreciate that."

"You're quite welcome." Denise smiled but wanted to sigh when she heard her pager buzzing. She quickly left the room, went back down to the nurses' station and called the switchboard. "This is Denise."

"Hi. You have a call waiting from Agatha Bowman's son. He asked for Mr. Hunter, but when I told him Mr. Hunter was on another call, he asked for the next person in charge."

"Good grief," Denise said before realizing it. "Okay, just give me about five minutes to get back up to my office, and you can put him through."

"No problem."

Denise could only imagine what Agatha had told her son, and she hoped he wasn't preparing to ream her. It had only been a towel for God's sake.

When the phone rang, she sat behind her desk and answered it. "This is Denise Shaw. How can I help you?"

"Hi, this is Mark Bowman, and thank you for taking my call. Also, is it Miss or Mrs.?"

"Mrs., but please call me Denise."

"That'll be fine, and you can call me Mark. The reason I'm contacting you is because I just received a call from my mother.

She was complaining about the staff and says the place isn't very well kept."

"I'm really sorry about your mother's experience, but—"

Mark interrupted her. "Please. There's really no need to apologize."

"I'm not sure I understand."

"Well, to put it plainly, when my mother makes any kind of threat, you should simply ignore her. She's been threatening people for years for one reason or another, but I'm very happy with your facility, and I know you're doing a great job."

Denise blew a quiet sigh of relief. "I'm glad you feel that way."

"My mother really is a nice woman, but right now she's upset about having to leave her home. She doesn't want to be there, so she's looking for anything she can to complain about."

"I understand."

"If I didn't run a corporation and have to travel for business as much as I do, I would move her in with my family. But you can see how that's just not possible. Not when she needs so much professional care."

Denise desperately wanted to tell him the truth: that his mother could still get around with a walker, she was still able to shower and dress herself, and with the exception of her forgetting a few things every now and then, there wasn't a lot wrong with her. She did need someone to cook for her, and while it wasn't a good idea for her to live alone, she definitely didn't need to be in a nursing facility. But Denise saw this all the time and knew it was best she keep her mouth shut.

"I understand, and your mother truly is in good hands."

"I believe that, and if you have any more trouble with her, please don't hesitate to call me."

"I will."

"Have a good day."

"You, too, Mark, and thanks for calling."

Denise hung up the phone and wondered if she'd now be able to get back to the résumés she'd been reviewing before having to stop and handle so many unexpected problems. But as soon as she'd finished her latest thought, her phone rang again.

"This is Denise speaking."

"Denise, it's Martha, up on five. I hate having to call you, but Hector's at it again."

Martha was the supervising nurse on the Alzheimer's floor, and Hector was known to remove his clothing on a moment's notice.

"Has he taken everything off?"

"Yes, and he's refusing to put anything back on. We even tried covering him up with a blanket, but every time we ease close to him, he swings at us violently."

"I'll be up there shortly."

"I hate bothering you, but since he always seems to calm down when you talk to him, I didn't know what else to do."

"It's fine, Martha. Really."

"Thanks."

Denise hung up the phone, leaned back in her chair, and placed both hands on top of her head. She sighed loudly and thought, "This job is going to be the death of me." If it weren't for the fact that she loved helping the elderly and she was so thankful to have a management position that paid her just over a hundred thousand dollars a year, she would submit her letter of resignation immediately. If she, Derrek, and Mackenzie hadn't gotten comfortably used to living a certain lifestyle and she and Derrek hadn't wanted to send Mackenzie to a top university, she would leave management altogether and go back to being a bedside nurse. Her love for taking care of older patients was the reason she'd left Covington Park Memorial five years ago and had signed on with the nursing home in the first place. She'd been so happy when she'd begun working there, but soon after, she'd been promoted to nursing supervisor and then two years ago to her current position. It was all a lot to be proud of and she was very grateful to have such an amazing career, but working sometimes ten- to fourteen-hour days, five days straight and then receiving calls from her staff members throughout most weekends was a heavy burden. Now, instead of being thrilled about having a successful career, she was always much happier when she was relaxing at home with her husband and daughter. Of course, there was also her father to consider because he would never be okay with her demoting herself. No, as far as Mr. Charles Theodore King was concerned, his daughter had to excel in every area of her life and strive for total perfection. She had to appear flawless, even though her father had hurtful secrets of his own.

Gosh, what she wouldn't give to have a little cocaine right now. Just one tiny line would do the trick, anything to help her through her day. Even better, she wished she could take some Vicodin—not one, the way she normally did, but two because last night she'd noticed that taking one hadn't done much for her at all. She knew it wouldn't be the smartest thing to do—not during working hours and on facility premises, but she was so on edge and needed something to calm her down as quickly as possible. She didn't want to do this but without thinking much more about it, she closed her door, pulled her purse from her left desk drawer, poured two pills into her hand, tossed them in her mouth, and drank some of the water sitting on her desk. Then, she waited a few minutes, exhaled, and headed up to the fifth floor to see about Hector.

Chapter 4

*I*t was five thirty, and while Denise could have easily worked a while longer, ten hours had been enough for one day. The morning had brought on one fire to put out after another, and the afternoon had only turned out worse. There had been phone call after phone call, two new admits, and also an impromptu meeting with Mr. Hunter, the marketing director, the CFO, and a few other managers. Normally, they met on Tuesdays, but since a couple of folks had booked outside appointments, Mr. Hunter had rescheduled the meeting for that afternoon. It hadn't taken long, but it had still added one more item to Denise's far too jam-packed list. She also wasn't happy about not getting another real chance to review more résumés the way she'd wanted.

She strolled over to her black Mercedes S550 and smiled when she saw Pamela backing her SUV out of her parking spot.

As Pamela drove closer to where Denise was standing, she rolled down her window and lowered the volume of her CD player. "What a busy, busy day."

"You're tellin' me. And it seems to get busier all the time. We need more people and fast."

"I agree, but maybe you'll have more time to work on that next week. Maybe even get a few interviews scheduled."

"I was hoping to do that today, but so much else was going on."

"I can help you if you want."

"If I don't read through those résumés pretty soon, I might have to take you up on that. We might even have to do it after hours or on a Saturday, if you're willing."

"Not a problem. Just let me know."

Denise leaned against her car. "So what are you doing this weekend?"

"Not a whole lot. I may drive up to Wisconsin tomorrow to see my folks, but on Sunday, I'm doing nothing. Just need a day to relax. What about you?"

"Pretty much the same. We'll likely visit my parents tomorrow and since we haven't been to church in a while, we're planning to do that on Sunday. After that, I'm hoping to rest."

"I hear you. Oh and thanks again for coming up to Agatha's room this morning. You never should have had to do that. She could have easily told me about some dirty towel."

"I know, but it was pretty clear that she wasn't going to be satisfied until she saw Mr. Hunter."

"Unreal. Okay, well, I guess I'd better get going. See ya on Monday."

"Enjoy your weekend."

Pamela drove away, and Denise sat inside her car. She pressed the Start button and considered whether she should call her guy. Thankfully, the two Vicodin she'd taken earlier had worked wonderfully, and interestingly enough, she didn't feel overly relaxed like she'd been expecting. She still felt calm even now, but she wasn't sure she had enough Vicodin or coke to get her through the next few days. She decided it was better to be safe, though, and dialed Butch.

"What's up?" he answered.

"Hey. Can you meet?"

"When?"

"In about thirty minutes?"

"I think I can do that. Same place?"

"Yes."

"See you then."

Denise pushed the XM radio button and chose the Heart and Soul Channel. A song by Ledisi was playing, so she left it there, put on her sunglasses and drove out of the parking lot. It was a gorgeous, sunny autumn afternoon, and Denise loved the changing of seasons. As she coasted down the rural road, she admired all the different leaf colors. Some were reddish, some orange, some brown, some yellow. She also saw a few evergreens that never lost their color. She was so at peace and looked forward to having a fabulous and very calm weekend.

She drove about ten minutes before stopping at a bank ATM drive-thru. She rarely kept a lot of cash on her, but of course, cash was the only form of payment Butch accepted. She didn't mind, though, because it wasn't like she would ever write a check to a drug dealer. As it was, she'd never even gone to his house because she didn't want to take a chance on having anyone connecting her with him.

When the machine dispensed twenty-five twenty-dollar bills, she stuck them in her purse and drove away. Her normal buy from Butch would only cost three hundred, but since she was withdrawing money, she figured she might as well withdraw a little more to keep in her wallet.

As she accelerated and changed lanes, Derrek called her.

She pushed the Talk button on the console of the car, so she could speak hands-free. "Hey, honey."

"Hi, baby. You off?"

"Yep, and boy what a day it was."

"That bad, huh?"

"And then some."

"I hate how stressed you always are."

"Me, too, but there's not a lot I can do about it."

"You could go back to bedside nursing any time you want."

"I was thinking about that earlier, but in order to earn the same money, I'd have to work just as many hours plus every other weekend."

"But you seemed so much happier then. You worked a lot of hours, but you never had to bring work home. You also never had to be on call. Plus, I make more than enough money to make up the difference if you wanted to work just forty hours."

"You're singing to the choir. But I just can't imagine giving up a top position. It would almost be like saying I couldn't cut it, and I gave up."

"Everyone knows you're not a quitter, and you shouldn't have to feel bad about doing what you love. There's nothing wrong with that."

"Once I get my staff replenished, things will run a lot smoother, and I won't have as much to worry about. It'll get better."

"I sure hope so, because you seem so tense lately."

"I'll be fine. So how was your day?"

"Good. It was busy, but nothing to complain about. I'm actually heading home pretty soon here."

"I have to pick up Mac in an hour and a half, so I'm running a few errands before then. I need to get a few toiletry items."

"What are we eating tonight?"

"Whatever you want is fine."

"I'll think about it."

"I'll see you later then. Love you."

"Love you, too."

Denise hated keeping secrets from her husband, but there was no way she could tell him the truth about where she was going. He would never understand, and there was no reason in the world to upset him. Especially over nothing.

After another fifteen minutes, Denise curved her vehicle through the park until she saw Butch's shiny, black, chrome-rimmed Escalade. It was almost identical to Derrek's. Denise pulled up beside him and Butch got out. Butch was Idris Elba handsome, but he also looked hardcore. Like he knew the streets inside out and wasn't someone to be played with. He also didn't speak like most thugs or dealers she'd seen on TV, and she liked that about him as well. He was a bad boy, no doubt about it, but he was smart, ridiculously charming, and never cursed.

"Hey, beautiful."

"Hey, how's it goin'?"

He passed a brown bag through her window. "Couldn't be better. You on the other hand, look a bit tired."

"I am," she said, thinking about how little sleep she was getting each night, which she knew was a result of her cocaine use. "I had a really long day."

"Well, that's even more the reason you'll be thanking me the next time I see you."

"Meaning?"

"I packed your two grams of coke and a nice size bag of Vs, but I also gave you a little something else. Something that will relax you even more than the Vicodin."

Denise wasn't sure she liked the sound of that. "I don't know."

"Just try it. Free of charge."

"What is it?"

"Dilaudid. In the pill form."

Denise knew full well what Dilaudid was because they'd used it quite often during her six-month stint in the ER. It had been her first year working as a nurse, and while they'd only administered it to patients who were experiencing excruciating pain, they'd always given it intravenously. Dilaudid was a powerful drug, a synthetic form of morphine, but she knew the pill version wouldn't work as quickly—not when it came to the way it made you feel emotionally, anyway. Still, while her gut told her she shouldn't accept anything other than what she'd come for, she didn't pull out the Dilaudid and give it back to him. Instead, she passed him fifteen twenties.

"See you, beautiful."

"Thanks for coming."

She pressed the button, putting up her window, and Butch strutted back to his vehicle. Denise watched him and for the first time, she felt strange. For some odd reason, she also thought about her parents. What would they think if they knew she was meeting a drug dealer in the middle of nowhere? For that matter, what would her best friend, Michelle, think or her boss and co-workers? She knew she wasn't like most of Butch's customers, people who were struggling with addiction and those who didn't know how they were going to pay for their next fix, but she also didn't like lying to Derrek the way she had earlier—not to mention, she'd lied to her daughter last night about having to skip out on the movie to do some work when she hadn't brought any work files home to begin with. Thankfully, she'd purchased enough coke to last her a couple of weeks, and she wouldn't have to meet up with Butch any time before that. If she was lucky, she had enough to last even longer.

Chapter 5

Denise cruised back through the park and exited onto the main street, heading to Mackenzie's junior high school. Minutes later, her phone rang. She smiled when she saw it was Michelle. Beautiful, wise, and always kind to everyone, Michelle was by far the best friend Denise had ever had.

"Hey girl, I was just thinking about you earlier," Denise said.

"We haven't chatted in a couple of days, and that's definitely out of the ordinary."

"I know. I thought about calling you from work, but I never got time."

"We should try to go to lunch next week."

"That would be great if I can break away. Normally, I'm so busy, I end up skipping it altogether."

"Not good," Michelle said.

"Tell me about it."

"So where are you now?"

"Um...on my way to pick up Mac from debate practice. I just got off work."

"Oh, okay. I just got off myself."

"So how are you enjoying your new job?" Michelle worked for an auto manufacturing supplier and had recently been promoted to marketing manager.

"I absolutely love it. It's everything I dreamed it would be."

"You've deserved that job for a long time, and I'm so happy for you."

"Thanks. It took me a while, but I think getting my master's last year really paid off."

"I'm sure it did."

"One of the other candidates still isn't happy about me being chosen, though."

"The woman you told me about a few months ago?"

"Yeah. She was already upset about not getting the promotion, but yesterday, my boss placed her on my team."

"So she reports to you now?"

"Yep."

"Oh no."

"'Oh no' is right. I just hope she eventually accepts the idea or decides to go work for another company. It's hard having someone work for you, when they resent you so much."

"Been there and done that, so I know how you feel. But hey, isn't your date with Eric tomorrow?"

"It is."

"Are you excited?"

"I am, and I'm so glad he decided to come introduce himself to me after church last Sunday."

"And he did it while you were talking to Derrek and me and a couple of other members, so he definitely wanted to get your number. He wasn't afraid to pull you away at all."

"He seems very nice, and he works as a business consultant for a major insurance company downtown."

"Has he ever been married?"

"Yes, but his divorce was finalized a year ago. He also doesn't have any children."

"I hope your date goes well. If it does, the four of us will have to go out sometime."

"For sure."

Denise and Michelle chatted for another five minutes. But as she accelerated, barely beating a stop signal, a state policeman tailed her and flashed his red lights. Denise knew he wanted her to pull over, and her heart practically thumped out of her chest.

"Hey girl, I need to run inside the store," she lied, "so let me call you back, okay?"

"Sounds good. Talk to you later."

Denise ended the call. *Oh my God, what if he searches my car?*

She was terrified, but she kept her cool, pulled over to the side of the road and watched the officer through her rearview mirror. He didn't get out of his vehicle right way, so she knew he was probably running her plates. While he did, she carefully removed the bag of goodies from her purse without any full-body movement and slipped them under her seat. Thank goodness for long arms.

She sat and waited, but the more time the officer took, the more she panicked. Her heart raced faster and a chill whipped through her insides. Had she maybe ran the red light after all? Had she possibly been speeding? Or what if he'd seen her meeting with Butch in the park, exchanging money for drugs with him? What if he'd witnessed the entire transaction?

Finally, after another minute or so, the tall, muscular, officer stepped out, slid on his hat, and started toward her. When he arrived at the side of her car, she let her window down.

"Good evening. I'll need to see your license, registration, and proof of insurance, please."

Denise reached inside her purse and removed her license. Then, she opened the glove box and pulled out the other two items.

The officer looked everything over. "Were you aware that one of your taillights is out? I noticed it when you stopped at the intersection a couple of blocks ago."

Denise exhaled cautiously and prayed this was all he wanted with her. "No, I wasn't. I had no idea."

"You should try to get that taken care of as soon as possible."

"I will, and thank you for letting me know."

The officer passed her information back to her, smiled and tipped his hat. "Have a nice day."

"You, too, Officer, and thank you again."

As he walked away, Denise breathed a huge sigh of relief. What a close call that had been, and she couldn't remember ever feeling more afraid of anything. Maybe it was best she not meet Butch again or buy drugs period. It wasn't like she desperately needed any of what she'd purchased from him, and she couldn't imagine what would happen to her, Derrek, and God help her, Mackenzie, if she was ever arrested and charged with possession. What a horrifying thought. She decided right then and there that, after finishing the stash she had now, she would be done with cocaine and Vicodin for good. She enjoyed the way both drugs made her feel, but they just weren't worth ruining her life or her family's. She would never knowingly cause pain and humiliation for her husband, daughter, or parents, so this was one wake-up call she couldn't and wouldn't ignore.

Denise was proud of her decision and glad she'd had such an amazing revelation before it was too late. She'd always known she could stop taking pills or snorting cocaine any time she wanted. She'd known this to be true all along, but it felt good finally being able to prove it.

All was good now, so Denise pulled herself together and went to pick up Mackenzie.

Chapter 6

Derrek pressed the four-digit code, disarming the security system, and walked over to the kitchen counter. There, he set down his briefcase and today's mail, and removed his blazer. He was glad to be home and ready to enjoy a weekend of rest and football. He knew they would likely go to church on Sunday, but tomorrow he would spend part of the day in front of the TV watching the college players and then on Sunday afternoon and evening he'd watch NFL games.

As he loosened his tie, he strolled through the house and walked upstairs. However, when he walked inside the master bedroom, the phone rang. He stepped closer to the nightstand and shook his head. It was Dixon again. Derrek stared at the lighted display and decided it was finally time he gave Dixon a piece of his mind.

He grabbed the phone from its base in a huff. "Look, Dixon!"

But all Derrek heard was a dial tone. He'd answered too late, and since it was obvious that Dixon wasn't going to stop calling until he spoke to him, he realized setting him straight once and for all was inevitable, and was the only way he wouldn't have to hear from his brother again.

Derrek removed his tie, unbuttoned his snow-white dress

shirt, and slipped off his pants. He went into the bathroom, turned on the shower, and tossed a large towel over the top of it. When he stepped inside, the hot, steamy water streamed across the front of his body. He savored every second of it and didn't want it to end. Over the last few days, his muscles had felt a bit tired and sore, but he knew it was only because he hadn't worked out in a couple of weeks. This was so out of the ordinary for him, but with his current work schedule, he just hadn't made time for it.

He stood still, but when he turned around, the phone rang. He wondered if it was his brother again and just thinking about the possibility of it, quickly ruined the peaceful vibe he was experiencing. Now, Derrek was to the point where he wanted this to end, and he couldn't wait to finish his shower, so he could call Dixon back. Enough was enough, and this would be the last day he'd ever have to deal with him.

Minutes later, Derrek dried his body, swiped deodorant under his arms, and got dressed. He had a taste for burgers and fries, so he pulled on a pair of jeans and slipped a V-neck cashmere sweater over his head. Denise wasn't a huge lover of beef, but he knew Mackenzie would be thrilled because she loved a great, juicy burger as much as he did. But as he went over to the phone, he realized all of this was the least of his worries because the red voicemail indicator light was flashing. Had Dixon actually left a message this time? If so, Derrek could only imagine the lame story or apology he'd rattled off, and he almost dreaded having to listen to it. Still, he dialed into the system and braced himself.

"Uh, D, it's me...your brother," he said, calling him by the nickname he'd used for Derrek since they were small boys. "I know it's been a long time, man, but I guess I should just begin by saying I'm sorry. I'm sorrier than you could possibly ever know, and I was wrong. I also know that no matter how many times I apologize, I'll never be able to make things up to you, but one thing has never changed: I still love you, man. I've always loved you, and I've missed you. I've wanted to call you, but whenever I tried to build up the nerve, I lost it. I knew how angry you were, and I just couldn't take a chance on how you might react."

Dixon paused for a couple of seconds, and it was then that Derrek realized how weak his brother sounded.

"The reason I've been calling you over the last few days, though, D, is because I've been diagnosed with pancreatic cancer. It's not good, and I'm in the hospital."

Derrek dropped down on the edge of the bed. His hand shook uncontrollably. He could barely steady the phone.

"I was hoping to tell you this before now, but can you call me? I really need to talk to you. I really need to hear your voice."

Derrek pressed the End button and held the phone with both hands. *Pancreatic cancer? Couldn't be.* Derrek sat holding the phone for a while longer and finally pushed the Caller ID button until he found Dixon's number.

"Hello?" Dixon answered shortly thereafter, speaking just above a whisper.

"Hey, how are you?"

"Not good, but I'm so glad you called."

"I'm sorry to hear the news."

Derrek waited for Dixon to say something else, but he didn't. The mere thought of them being on the phone after all this time was beyond awkward, so Derrek didn't say anything, either.

"D," Dixon finally said. "I really am sorry about everything. I'm sorry about all the lies I told over the years, I'm sorry about never paying you the way I promised, and I'm especially sorry about that five thousand dollars. To be honest, I had no justification for borrowing that kind of money from you and not paying it back, but D, I was pretty angry and hurt back then. You never knew this, but right after I borrowed the money, I found out I had prostate cancer. The doctor caught it early, but I was so upset that I felt like it was only right for me to enjoy the one vacation I'd always wanted to go on. And while I know it was wrong, I was so angry about my illness, I actually resented you for asking for your money back. I was thinking like a crazy man, and the way I saw it was that you and your family had the rest of your lives ahead of you, but I might get cancer again and die in a second."

Derrek was speechless.

"But I hope you believe me when I say I wasn't myself. I was acting on a level of insanity, but if I had it to do over again..."

"And how long have you been sick this time?"

"A couple of months... but when my doctor discovered it, I was already at stage four."

Derrek swallowed hard, tears rolling down his cheeks. "Man, why didn't you leave a message all those other times you called?"

"I didn't think you would call me back, so I just kept hoping that eventually you would pick up and I could talk to you directly. But today I realized it was probably best that I leave a message because now I know for sure I'm not going to get better."

"Dixon, I'm so sorry to hear this."

"It's life, D."

"I know but this is a very hard pill to swallow."

"You can say that again, but there is something I need to know."

"What is it?"

"Can you somehow find it in your heart to forgive me?"

Tears flowed heavily from Derrek's eyes. "I forgive you completely."

"Thank you. I really needed to hear that, and if I can ask you just one final favor, will you come see me?"

"Of course. What hospital are you in?"

"The one we were born in." He slightly chuckled. "Can you believe that?"

"Wow."

"Can you come this evening?"

"I'll be there as soon as Denise and Mac get home."

"I can't wait to see all of you. I'd better go now, though."

"I love you, Dixon."

"I love you, D. I always will no matter what."

Derrek set the phone down, sobbing like never before. "Dear...God...What have I done? Please...please...please... I'm begging you...Please don't take my brother. Not now."

Derrek cried for a few minutes, wiped his face with his hands, and then went into the bathroom. He turned on the faucet, ran a small towel under it, and washed his face with cold water. Then he stood, gazing into the mirror at bloodshot eyes, and tears welled up in them again. He'd done a terrible thing. Three years ago, he'd written off his brother because of money, and now he didn't know whether Dixon had three months to live. What if they never got a chance to spend any real time together? Derrek was devastated, and just as he wiped his face again, Denise walked into the bathroom. He wanted to tell her what was going on, but instead, he grabbed her in his arms, squeezing her as tightly as he could, and prayed for God to heal his brother.

Chapter 7

*E*ven though Derrek worked at a hospital, it was tough having to walk inside this one because being there had nothing to do with business. He was there to see his terminally ill brother, and he could hardly fathom the whole idea of it. An hour had passed since Derrek had spoken to Dixon, but he was still very heartbroken, confused, and numb. He was filled with loads of regret, and no matter how much he tried he couldn't shake any of it.

Derrek, Denise, and Mackenzie pushed through the revolving door and over to the information desk.

A silver-haired, distinguished-looking gentleman smiled at them. "How may I help you?"

"We're here to see my brother, Dixon Shaw, but we don't know the room number."

"No problem." The man typed a few keystrokes on his keyboard, looked at the computer screen, and wrote Dixon's room number on a small sheet of paper. "He's on the eighth floor."

Derrek took the information. "Thank you."

As they proceeded down the main corridor, no one spoke, and soon they turned left and waited for the elevator. When it arrived, they stepped inside, and Derrek pressed the eighth-floor button. Thankfully, there were no stops in between, and now they walked down the long hallway to Dixon's room. Derrek was a nervous wreck, but suddenly, all he could think about was Dixon recovering. Maybe he could beat the cancer after all. He'd heard Dixon very clearly when he'd said his cancer was in its final stage, but he also knew that God could perform an amazing miracle. He knew anything was possible, and he'd certainly met a number of patients where he worked who'd beaten stage-four illnesses a while ago, and they were still in remission today. He did know that the overall survival rate for pancreatic cancer was pretty dismal, but he still hoped, wished, and prayed that his brother's outcome would be different.

They strolled past the oncology nurses' station, perusing various room numbers. However, when they stopped in front of Dixon's room, Derrek saw an attractive, thirty-something woman with short hair standing outside of it. Dixon's best friend, Sam, was there, too, but since the door was closed, Derrek wondered what was going on.

Sam, who after all these years still looked the same, stocky and bald, immediately shook Derrek's hand and hugged him. "It's been a long time, D, and I'm glad you came." Then he spoke to Denise and Mackenzie. "I also want you guys to meet Dixon's fiancée, Nina."

Denise smiled. "Hi Nina, it's good to meet you."

Derrek and Mackenzie said hello, too, and then Derrek asked, "So what's going on? Why is the door closed?"

Sam seemed as though he hated to answer. "About twenty minutes ago, Dixon complained of some numbness and now they believe he's had a stroke. It all happened so fast."

"I was just on the phone with him."

Nina folded her arms. "We know. We were in the room with him. As a matter of fact, I was in the room with him every time he called you. He's called you almost every day since the doctor admitted him."

Derrek could tell Nina wasn't too happy with him, and now he felt worse. He also still worried about what was going on in Dixon's room because while he could hear voices, he couldn't make out any of what they were saying. He wished someone would come and tell them something. Anything.

After about another five minutes of all of them standing around in total silence, the door opened, and the attending physician walked out, looking at Sam and Nina. "Let's walk down to one of the conference rooms, so I can give you an update."

"This is Dixon's twin brother, sister-in-law, and niece," Sam told him.

"I'm Dr. Freemont," he said, shaking their hands. "Very nice to meet all of you."

They followed the doctor and after entering the room, they sat around the table.

Dr. Freemont closed the door and sighed. "I wish I had better news, but Dixon has definitely had a stroke. He's completely paralyzed on his left side, and he can no longer speak. He mumbled a couple of times, but that's about as much as he can do."

Tears seeped from Nina's eyes, and Denise and Mackenzie wiped their faces, too.

"I'm truly very sorry," Dr. Freemont continued. "But based on the noticeable decrease in his heart rate and blood pressure, he may have twenty-four hours at the most."

Derrek's hands shook worse than they had when he'd been listening to Dixon's voice message. "Isn't there anything that can be done?"

"No, unfortunately not. We finished the last possible round of chemo last month, and in terms of life support, Dixon signed a do-not-resuscitate order when he was admitted."

Derrek broke into a cold sweat and struggled to breathe. Denise wrapped her arm around him.

Dr. Freemont patted Derrek on the shoulder. "I'm really sorry about your brother." Then he turned to Nina and Sam. "I'm sorry to have to share this kind of news with all of you."

Sam blinked back tears. "We appreciate everything you've tried to do."

"I wish we could have done more. Our job now, though, is to make Dixon as comfortable as possible and once the nurses get him a little more situated, you can go in to see him."

They all thanked Dr. Freemont, and he left the room.

Nina slid her chair back, stood up and tossed Derrek a dirty look. "This is all your fault."

Derrek quickly noticed all the shocked faces but said, "Excuse me?"

Sam got to his feet. "Nina, please. This isn't the time for this."

"No, I think it's the perfect time because if Dixon hadn't been so hurt and worried about trying to make amends with his brother, he wouldn't have deteriorated so quickly." She stared at Sam and then snarled her nose at Derrek. "He talked about you all the time over these last three years and that irritated me enough, but then when he came to the hospital last week, all he thought about was trying to contact you."

"I know, and I can't apologize enough. I'm very sorry."

"Yeah, I'm sorry, too. Sorry you ever showed up here," she said, leaving the room.

Sam seemed embarrassed. "D, she's only lashing out at you because of how hurt she is."

"I understand," Derrek said, but deep down a mountain of

guilt gnawed at his heart and consumed his soul. This just couldn't be happening, he thought, resting his elbows onto the table and laying his face inside the palm of his hands.

Sam touched his shoulder. "Everything is going to be okay. I should go check on Nina, though."

When Sam left, Derrek turned toward Denise. "Can you believe this? Can you believe I let this thing happen? I mean, my brother is dying, baby."

Denise pulled him closer. "Honey, I'm sorry."

Mackenzie leaned her head against his shoulder. "I'm sorry, too, Daddy. I'm sorry for all of us."

A half hour passed, and Derrek, Denise, and Mackenzie finally walked in to see Dixon. Nina looked over at the three of them, kissed Dixon on the cheek and brushed by them on her way out. Sam patted Dixon's leg and left the room as well, and Derrek walked up to the bed. Dixon had lost a lot of weight, his skin was pale, and his hair was gone, but Derrek still recognized his brother. He still saw his own features, and it was amazing how none of that had changed.

Denise went to the other side of the bed and kissed Dixon on the forehead. "How are you, brother-in-law? It's so good to see you, and we all love you so very much."

"We really, really do, Uncle Dixon." Mackenzie reached for his right hand, and Dixon squeezed it. He also grunted several words, but since he couldn't open his mouth, they couldn't understand him. This whole scene was killing Derrek. His spirit broke completely.

Denise smiled at her brother-in-law and kissed him again. "Dixon, Mac and I are going to be right outside, okay?"

Dixon tried to speak again, and now Derrek knew that not only could he hear them, he understood what they were saying.

"We'll be in the waiting area," Denise told her husband and embraced her daughter as they went into the hallway.

Derrek grabbed his brother's hand. "Dixon, if you can hear me squeeze my hand."

Dixon squeezed it.

"Gosh, I have so much I wanna say, but mostly I want you to know how sorry I am for letting money come between us. I wasn't happy about what you did, but now if it would mean making you well, I would give you every dime I have. I would do anything, Dixon, you hear me?"

Dixon squeezed his hand.

"I also need to know that you forgive me. If you do, Dixon, please squeeze my hand again."

Dixon clutched his hand but longer this time.

"We've been through so much together. Good times and bad, but I'm glad you're my brother. We had a hard life early on, but Grandma and Grandpa turned everything around for us. We went from starving to eating three home-cooked meals a day. We went from not having our own school supplies to having enough to share with others. Remember?"

Dixon squeezed his hand, and tears rolled down Derrek's face.

"Oh God, please save my brother, please give us just a little more time together. I'm begging You."

Derrek held his eyes closed tight but when he opened them, he saw a single tear flowing down each side of Dixon's face.

"I love you, man. I always have, I always will, and that will never change."

Dixon mumbled a few words in the back of his throat, squeezed Derrek's hand and tears flowed onto his pillow.

Derrek squeezed Dixon's hand, too, praying this was nothing more than a cruel nightmare.

Chapter 8

The longest hour in history had passed and since there had been no noticeable change, Derrek sat sobbing like a five-year-old. Denise had never seen him so upset, and she could barely stand it. So much so that she did all she could not to burst into tears herself. When Derrek's grandfather and grandmother had passed a couple of years apart, Denise had witnessed Derrek crying then, too, but this was different. The news about his brother was tearing him in two, and she'd never seen him suffer so intensely— not even when he'd broken down and given graphic details about his parents and their drug using. He'd shed tears, but again, it hadn't been anything compared to what she was witnessing now.

It was too much for her because when Derrek hurt, she hurt. It was also difficult knowing what she knew because of her nursing background. She'd seen lots of cancer and stroke patients, both when she'd worked at the hospital and now at the nursing home, and unless God decided differently, she knew her brother-in-law was in fact going to die. She also knew it would happen in twenty-four hours or less just the way Dr. Freemont had mentioned, but she didn't dare admit that to Derrek. She could tell that, on the one hand, he knew what the truth was, but on the other, he wanted to believe there was a chance of survival. He was hoping he and Dixon would have another opportunity at brotherhood. Denise hoped that, too, because the last thing she wanted was to lose her brother-in-law, but it was her medical experience that forced her to accept reality. Sometimes she hated that, but it was just the way things were.

Denise sat for as long as she could, but when her nerves couldn't take all the tears and sad faces anymore, she got up and strode down to the restroom. Once inside, she hurried into the middle stall, quickly pulled out a bottle of water she'd taken from the refrigerator just before leaving home and then popped a couple of Vicodin. She washed them down with three large swigs, placed the bottle back in her purse and leaned her head against the wall. Her stomach was empty, so she knew she'd be feeling a lot better about things very soon and would be much better equipped to be there for her husband the way he needed her to.

She leaned her entire body against the wall with her eyes closed. She didn't want to leave the stall just yet, but she also didn't want to appear to be gone too long. So, she opened the door. When, she did, however, Nina entered the restroom. She and Denise locked eyes but didn't say anything. Denise wasn't sure what to do next but then realized it was best that she at least wash her hands, making it seem that she really was in there for the right reason. Nina went into a different stall, but when she came out Denise started to leave, until Nina stopped her.

"I want to apologize for the way I spoke to your husband. I didn't mean any of what I said, but it just seems that ever since Dixon was diagnosed I've been looking for someone to blame. I know it's not right, but when I saw Derrek, I lost it."

"We all grieve differently, and I understand."

Nina leaned her body against the vanity top. "I think I took my anger out on your husband because Dixon would always say that as soon as he made things right with him, we could get married. It never made any sense to me, but that's how he felt."

"Gosh, I had no idea. I'm sorry to hear that."

"He wanted to repay him, and he wanted him to be at our ceremony...but now it's too late for any of that."

Denise hugged her.

"This has been the toughest three months of my life," Nina said, "and none of it seems real."

"How did Dixon know something was wrong? What made him go to the doctor?"

"At first he started losing weight, and then he seemed so tired all the time. But when he started having major digestive problems, that's when he made an appointment."

"That's the thing about pancreatic cancer," Denise said, "it can progress and spread well before a person has any symptoms."

"When we found out it was stage four, I thought I would die. I just didn't want to believe it. I still don't."

"It's hard for me, too. So very sad and very shocking."

"The other thing is that by the time he was diagnosed, the cancer had already spread to his stomach and bones."

Denise shook her head, totally at a loss for words.

Nina washed her hands. "I'm really glad Derrek finally called Dixon back because it really made his day. When they hung up, the first thing he said was, 'My brother forgives me, and he's coming to see me.'"

"I'm glad, too."

"If you wanna know the truth, I believe that's why he held on for as long as he did this week."

Denise and Nina finally left the restroom. They chatted all the way back to the waiting area where Derrek, Mackenzie, and Sam sat quietly.

Nina took a seat next to Derrek. "I'm sorry for everything I said. This has been a very difficult time for me, but I had no right speaking to you the way I did."

"No, I'm the one who's sorry, so please don't worry about it."

Denise sat on the other side of Derrek and rested her hand on his thigh. "So, are the nurses still in with Dixon?"

"Yes, but we should be able to go back in very soon."

Denise turned to her daughter. "Mac, honey, how are you holding up?"

"I'm fine, Mom. Just a little hungry."

"I'm sure the cafeteria is closed, but we can always drive over to one of the fast-food restaurants across the street. I also need to call Mom and Dad to let them know what's going on."

Both of them stood, and Denise continued, "Can we bring anything back for you guys?"

"No," they all replied.

"Okay, well, we won't be long."

Denise and Mackenzie walked around the corner to the elevator, but when the doors opened, Denise couldn't believe her eyes. She had only seen her father-in-law three times since marrying Derrek, but she knew it was him. His salt-and-pepper hair looked as though it hadn't been combed in a few days, his jean outfit didn't seem to have been washed recently, and one of his tennis shoes had a hole in it. Denise was sure this was the reason he looked at them and then quickly looked away as if he were ashamed. Still, he recognized Denise and spoke to her.

"It's good to see you, daughter-in-law."

"It's good to see you, too, Dad." She called him that because this was what he'd asked her to do the first time she'd met him. Derrek, of course, hadn't liked it.

Mr. Shaw glanced over at Mackenzie again. "Is this my beautiful granddaughter?"

"Yes," Denise said, smiling.

"Hi, Grandpa."

Denise was very proud of her daughter for treating her grand-father with the utmost respect, even though she barely knew him. She did worry, however, how Derrek might react because there was just no telling.

"Everyone is in the waiting area," she told him, "so we'll walk back around there with you."

Denise and Mackenzie followed him, and as soon as Sam saw Mr. Shaw he walked over to him. It was clear they'd seen each other recently.

"How's it going, Mr. Shaw?"

"As well as can be expected I guess. How's Dixon?"

"Not too good."

Mr. Shaw's face turned grim. Still he walked over to Nina. "You hangin' in there?"

"I'm trying to, Dad."

Denise was a little shocked to hear Nina calling him Dad, too, and this could only mean one thing: Dixon had made contact with his father at some point after he and Derrek had stopped speaking. For years, neither of them would have anything to do with their parents because whenever they saw them, they usu-ally asked for drug money, but apparently Dixon had undergone a change of heart.

There was silence but then Mr. Shaw faced Derrek, who was still sitting down. "Hi, son."

Derrek stared at him blankly but then looked away. Mr. Shaw must have known it wasn't a good idea to press the issue because he then said to Sam, "Are they allowing Dixon to have visitors?"

"Yes, but the nurses were in there. We can go check to see if it's okay to go in, though."

As Sam and Mr. Shaw went on their way, Denise looked at her husband who pretended his long-lost father didn't exist. Derrek watched the HD TV mounted on the wall, acting as if nothing had happened.

"Honey, why don't you ride with Mac and me to get something to eat? I think it would be good to get some fresh air."

"No, I wanna go back in to see Dixon as soon as I can."

Denise agreed with him wholeheartedly and didn't think it was a good idea for him to leave the hospital, either, but she also feared what he might say to his father if he approached Derrek again. Mackenzie must have sensed her concern. "Mom, we don't have to go if you don't want to. I can get some chips and a soda."

"Sweetie, are you sure?"

"Yes," she whispered. "I don't think we should leave Daddy right now."

Denise hugged her daughter, and Mackenzie strolled around to the elevator. Then Denise sat next to Derrek, praying he wouldn't make a scene before the night was over. She hoped with all her might that her father-in-law would leave the hospital as soon as he visited Dixon.

Chapter 9

With weary eyes, Derrek relaxed farther into his chair, resting his head against the wall. What a day. What a truly depressing and dreadful experience, not to mention he had more regrets than most people could combine in a lifetime. He'd been thinking about a number of things he could have handled differently, but the one that stuck in his mind the most was the fact that he'd literally ended his relationship with his brother over money— a worldly possession that should never supersede family. Yes, Dixon had been wrong for taking advantage of him the way he had for so many years, and Derrek doubted anyone would be okay with loaning five thousand dollars to a family member and then have them make no attempt to pay it back, but Derrek still wished he'd forgiven him before today. He wished he'd tried to work things out with Dixon from the very beginning. Although, that was the thing about hoping, wishing, and praying after the fact—it was usually too late in most cases, and Dixon's terminal diagnosis had proven that.

But Derrek knew he could go on and on with his coulda-shoulda-woulda philosophy, yet it would never change anything. It would never alter reality or the future, and now he had to figure out a way to live with it.

Then, adding insult to injury, his no-good father had shown up. Derrek couldn't remember the last time he'd seen him, but what he did know was that it hadn't been long enough. He despised everything about the man, and he also wondered how he'd known Dixon was ill, let alone in the hospital. Maybe Dixon had found a way to get in touch with him once he'd learned about his cancer, but either way, Derrek wanted nothing to do with him. Not today, not tomorrow, not twenty years from now, and his feeling was the same regarding his mother. He'd heard a year ago that she was living in some awful housing complex and that she slept with multiple men per week for drugs, and he would never subject his daughter to that kind of grandmother. Denise didn't agree with him and thought he should at least try to get his parents into rehab, but Derrek didn't see why he should have to be responsible for parents who hadn't cared about him. It didn't make any sense, and he refused to consider it.

Derrek looked at Denise and grabbed her hand.

She smiled at him. "Do you wanna go see Dixon again?"

"Not while my father is in there." He spoke matter-of-factly and for whatever reason, the thought of his father standing over Dixon playing the loving, doting father to his dying son pissed Derrek off. It also took everything in him not to storm down the hallway and ask him the question of the hour: why? Derrek knew he and Dixon had come a long way since the age of eight and that God had blessed them to do okay in life, but the little boy in Derrek still wanted answers. The grown man he was today wanted to know how any father could leave and forsake his own twin boys like it was nothing—like he hadn't had any obligations to either of them. Didn't he know that every child needed and wanted to feel loved? Hadn't anyone told him that every son desperately needed his father?

The whole idea of what his father and mother had done made

Derrek ill, and it was going to take every ounce of restraint he could muster not to attack his father when he returned to that waiting area. It would take all the Christian values his grandparents had instilled in him not to go completely off on his father like a common enemy. He also knew this wasn't the place or time for family drama. He certainly didn't want to say or do anything that would disappoint or hurt Denise or Mackenzie.

When another twenty minutes passed, Sam and Mr. Shaw walked back into the waiting area.

Nina stood right away. "Are there any changes?"

Sam paused but then said, "His blood pressure has dropped a tad lower."

Nina looked at Derrek. "You wanna go in next?"

"No, you go ahead." Truthfully, Derrek did want to go see his brother now, but he also felt it was only right that Nina have as much time with Dixon as possible. After all, she'd been the one who had been there for him well before his diagnosis, and he could tell how hurt she was. It was clear how much she loved Dixon.

When Nina left, Mr. Shaw stood with his hands in his pockets, seemingly feeling out of place, but then said, "Son, can I talk to you for a minute?"

Derrek scowled at him and said nothing. He was so enraged, he was shocked no one saw smoke oozing from the top of his head.

"Son, I know I don't deserve any of your time, but I'd really like to talk to you."

Derrek tried but couldn't hold his tongue any longer. "Fine. Let's step outside."

"Honey, maybe you should go and spend a little more time with your brother first," Denise quickly added. "Then we can all walk out together."

"No, I'm gonna deal with this now."

Derrek headed around the corner and over to the elevator, never looking back at Denise. His father followed, but they didn't say a word while they waited, nor when they stepped inside the elevator, and not when they arrived on the main floor, either.

It was after they walked through the lobby and went outside to the parking lot that things got ugly.

"So what is it that you wanna talk about?" Derrek spat.

"Son, I just wanna apologize for everything. Your mother and I never did right by you boys, and I'm very sorry. Sorrier than you'll ever believe."

"That's the most pathetic thing I've ever heard. You know why? Because there's not a thing you could say that will make up for the way you treated us."

"Son, what about forgiveness? What about the fact that everyone makes mistakes, even you."

"Excuse me?"

"I'm just saying, nobody's perfect."

"You're a real piece of work, you know that? You bring your useless behind over to this hospital, acting like Father of the Year, and now you think you have the right to make comparisons? You're nothing like me! You're a no-good, deadbeat, drug addict who only cares about his next fix. And anyway . . . why are you even here?"

"Because Dixon asked me. He hired an investigator to find me when he found out he was sick."

Derrek laughed like a crazy man. "And I'm sure you couldn't wait to come a runnin', could you? I'll bet you were foaming at the mouth thinking how Dixon might just be leaving you a little money."

Mr. Shaw slowly shook his head. "Dear God, no. I'm here because I love my son. I love both of you boys."

"You must think I'm crazy."

"No, I don't think anything like that. I know you don't want to hear it, but no matter what happened...no matter how long I've been away, I never stopped loving either one of you."

"You're such a liar, and not even a good one."

"Son, what I did is in the past. I'll never be able to change that, but I'm trying my best to explain things now. Those drugs messed up everything, and I just couldn't see how to pull my way out."

Derrek rolled his eyes. "That's a bunch of crap, too, but let me ask you this. Even if *you* couldn't help getting caught up with drugs, why on earth did you have to drag our mother into it? Why couldn't you just leave her out of it?"

"Son, there's so much you don't know."

"I know enough."

"You really don't, so let's just leave it at that."

"We had a wonderful mother and had you not gotten her strung out, her life would have turned out so differently. You ruined her," he yelled. "You ruined all of us."

A few people had already strolled by them, but the man and woman passing now, peered at them strangely. Derrek was sorry to be acting this way in public, but he needed to speak his mind.

"Like I said, there's a lot you don't know."

Derrek threw his hands in the air. "Why do you keep saying that? Why are you trying to act as though you're not to blame for everything? Why won't you just tell the truth?"

Mr. Shaw raised his voice, too, for the first time. "You want the truth? Well, here it is: your wonderful mother is the one who strung *me* out!"

"What? So now you're going to lie on our mother just to make yourself look good? You're sick."

"Think whatever you want, but as God is my witness, I never touched one drug until your mother introduced me to them."

"Like I said . . . you're a liar and not even a good one. Now why don't you get the hell out of here?"

"Being angry with me, son, won't change the truth. And I just hope you can eventually forgive me."

"You know what? I came out here like you wanted, but now I'm finished with you for good. You hear me? I'm done, and as far as I'm concerned you're dead. You no longer exist."

"Son, please—" He started to say but Derrek's phone rang. It was Denise calling.

"Honey, Dixon's blood pressure has dropped pretty low, so it won't be long now."

Derrek held the phone, speechless. Then his heart dropped.

Chapter 10

$\mathcal{I}$t had all happened so quickly. Not just Dixon's death but everything leading up to it. Dixon had left Derrek a message, Derrek had called him back shortly thereafter, Derrek, Denise, and Mackenzie had gone over to the hospital, and now Dixon was gone. Not more than a few hours had passed from beginning to end, yet none of this seemed real. Certainly not to Derrek, of course, but Denise still couldn't fathom any of what had happened either: her brother-in-law had passed before turning forty. The loss of a loved one was never easy, but as Denise observed her husband from across the room, she could tell he was in a daze. She doubted he could hear any of what was being said, even though the house was pretty full, because all he did was stare into space.

Once the funeral home had picked up the body, Denise had insisted that Sam and Nina come back to their house, and Denise's parents had driven over, as well. Michelle was there also. They'd even ordered takeout from Derrek's favorite Mexican restaurant, although with the exception of Mackenzie and Denise's parents, no one had eaten very much. Derrek had never so much as gone into the kitchen, and Denise wondered what she could say or do to help him. She'd tried talking to him and consoling him the best way she knew how, but so far nothing was working.

Sam rested his elbows on his knees and clasped his hands together. He sat between Nina and Michelle on the sofa in the family room. "Gosh...I can't believe my best friend is gone. He's really, really gone."

Nina looked at him with tears streaming down her face but didn't say anything. Everyone else got quiet, too.

Denise wasn't sure what to say either, so she walked over to Derrek. "Honey, why don't you let me fix you something to eat? You haven't had a thing for hours."

Derrek shook his head, no, but never looked at her.

"What about something to drink?"

He shook his head again but barely.

He was deeply hurt, and Denise hated seeing him like this. He was in pretty bad shape, and she wasn't sure what it would take to lift his spirits. She knew the old phrase, "time heals all wounds," was true to a certain extent, but she wondered how much time it would in fact take for Derrek to accept the loss of his brother. More than that, she wondered how long it would take for him to forgive himself for not speaking to Dixon for years.

Wilma, Denise's mother, who had the looks and class of the amazing Nancy Wilson, stood up. "Denise, honey, do you want me to put the food away for you?"

"That would be great, Mom."

Mackenzie pushed herself up from the ottoman she was sitting on. "I'll help you, Granny."

"Me, too, Mom," Michelle said. Michelle had called Wilma Mom almost the entire time she'd been best friends with Denise. She looked as fabulous as always; her hair was cut short with not a strand out of place and her clothes fit her toned body perfectly.

Wilma smiled. "Good. I'll take all the help I can get."

"Is there anything I can do?" Charles asked his daughter. Denise's father was every bit of six-foot-three, and Denise didn't know of anyone who had a younger, finer looking dad in his sixties than she did.

"No, Daddy, but thanks."

"What about you, son?" he said to Derrek.

Charles waited for Derrek to respond, but all he did was nod his head and burst into tears.

Nina sniffled a couple of times herself and got to her feet. "Denise, can I speak to you privately?"

"Of course. Let's go in the study."

Nina followed her and as soon as they walked inside a room filled with three walls of built-in bookcases, Denise shut the door.

Nina stood silently for a few seconds, then began to weep again. Denise hugged her but wondered what was wrong. There was no question she was suffering a tremendous loss, but she seemed to be upset about something else, too.

"I know it hurts, but in time you'll start to feel better," Denise said.

Nina slightly pulled away. "Thank you for inviting me here because without Dixon, I'd be home alone. It's really hard not being near my parents and brothers in Boston, so I'm really glad to be here with all of you. Dixon's family."

"I understand, and we're here for you for as long as you need us."

"I really appreciate that," she said, sniffling. "The reason I wanted to talk to you is because even though I have a small life insurance policy on Dixon, I don't know how I'm going to pay for any upfront costs."

"No worries. We'll do whatever we need to."

"Are you sure?"

"Of course. Derrek wouldn't want it any other way."

"I can pay you back as soon as the check..." Her words trailed off and tears rolled again. "I'm sorry...but this is so embarrassing. Dixon and I have lived together all this time but we have nothing, Denise."

"It's okay. You don't have to explain anything."

"No, I feel like I have to tell you the truth. Especially, since I'm having to ask you for money and you don't even know me."

Denise leaned against the desk.

Nina breathed in and exhaled. "The reason we have no money is because Dixon was addicted to crack."

Denise covered her mouth. "Oh my God."

"He abused drugs for nearly two years but then earlier this year I told him that if he didn't get help, I was leaving. And thankfully, that's when he went to rehab."

"I'm stunned, Nina."

"I wanted to leave him so many times, but Denise I loved him so much and I just kept praying he would stop."

"Well, the good news is that he finally did."

"Yeah...but now he's dead. He's gone."

Nina began shedding more tears but then someone knocked on the door.

Denise strolled toward it. "Yes?"

It was her father. "Hey, I hate to interrupt, but I need to chat with you for a minute."

Nina started toward the door. "That's fine, Mr. King. We were pretty much finished, anyway."

When Nina shut the door behind her, Denise said, "What is it, Dad?"

"Look, I'm not sure what it's gonna take to snap your husband out of that funk he's in, but you need to have a talk with him. The two of you have a funeral to plan, and you can't do that if he's moping around crying like a baby. I've watched you over the last hour, and you've got to stop babying him, Denise. You've got to make him man up."

Denise's chest tightened, and she was mortified. Although she shouldn't have really been surprised because, sadly, this was the way her father had always been. The man had no compassion or sympathy for anyone who showed signs of weakness.

"You've got to pull yourself together," he continued before Denise could say anything. "You've got to stand up and be the strong woman I taught you to be and then push your husband out of this rut he's fallen in. Get him back on his feet. It's not like he'd even spoken to his brother for years anyhow, so life goes on."

"I know, Daddy, but Derrek is really having a tough time with this. He regrets not talking to his brother for all that time, and now Dixon is dead. But I'm sure he'll be fine."

"Your husband is weak just like his old man. I've always told you that, and seeing him the way he is tonight has finally confirmed it."

"Daddy, please try to understand."

"Well, I just hope he's not planning to do all that crying at the funeral because two of my closest friends will likely be there: the CEO where Derrek works and also one of the hospital board members. And I don't wanna be embarrassed."

Denise stared at her father but knew it wasn't worth trying to reason with him. He judged and criticized everyone, and all Denise wanted was for him to leave—leave the room so she could settle her racing nerves in peace. Her father always tended to have this effect on her. Thankfully, Mackenzie knocked at the door and opened it.

"Mom, Daddy just went upstairs, and he's so sad."

Denise faced her father. "Daddy, I have to go."

"That's fine, but just remember what I said."

Denise hurried up to the master bedroom, and the first thing she saw was Derrek sitting on the side of the bed, weeping.

She sat down and hugged him. "Honey, I know this is hard, and I'm so sorry."

"Baby...this...is...unbearable. It hurts so, so much."

"I know."

"Oh my God," he said, letting her go. "I'll never forgive myself for treating my brother so horribly."

Denise had known all along that this was the thought that had been eating away at Derrek.

"Why couldn't I have just answered the phone when he first started calling? And why didn't he call me when he first learned about his cancer?"

"I don't know, honey, but at least you got to talk to him today. At least both of you apologized and forgave each other."

Derrek got up and went over to the window, looking out at the backyard. "But it wasn't the same as if we'd made things right when he was well."

Denise walked up behind him. "Honey, why don't you lie down? You really need to rest."

"I can't. Baby, my brother is gone. He's dead, and there's nothing I can do about it. And you know what else?" he said, turning and looking at her. "I wish I were dead, too. A part of me is already gone, anyhow, so what difference will it make?"

"Honey, please. You can't mean that. What about Mackenzie and me?"

Derrek quickly moved away from her. "I'm sorry, but I need to get out of here."

"To go where?"

"I need this pain to go away."

"But leaving won't help anything."

"Baby, I can't handle this. I can't go the rest of the night feeling like this. So, I'll be back, okay?"

Denise could see in his eyes what he was planning, and while she didn't want Derrek knowing that she still used Vicodin and did cocaine, she knew she had to stop him from leaving the house. He was in no condition to drive, and what replayed over and over in her mind was his statement about wishing he were dead. She was pretty sure she knew him better than that—he clearly wasn't the suicidal type—but she also knew he wasn't himself right now. He wasn't thinking logically, and she had to do something.

"Baby, I know you're upset, but I have everything you need right here."

Derrek glared at her. This made her prepare for the worst, but to her surprise, all he said was, "Coke?"

"Yes."

"Where is it?"

She was thankful she'd brought her new stash inside the house and had put it away before heading to the hospital. "In the lower right-hand drawer."

Derrek never said a word and calmly sat down in the high-back chair. Denise strolled over to the armoire and pulled out a sandwich-size baggie and passed it to him. He didn't even ask for a straw to snort it with. He simply scooped out a tad of the powder with the tip of his finger, lifted it to his nose, and inhaled it. He did this twice, closed his eyes and leaned back into the chair. He acted as though he'd never felt better. He was happy, and that's all Denise wanted.

Chapter 11

A month had passed since the funeral and while Derrek had finally returned to work just a few days ago, he'd practically had to drag himself out of bed every day to go there. At first, he'd wondered if he'd ever feel well enough to go out of the house again, what with all the depression he'd been struggling with, but last week he'd decided it was best that he at least try to get back to some of his daily responsibilities. Still, though, with each passing hour he sometimes felt like dying, and he could now officially say that he'd never felt more hopeless. He just couldn't shake his regretful feelings about Dixon or accept the fact that he simply hadn't been there for his brother the way he should have. He'd severed ties with him because of money, one of the main things Derrek still couldn't get beyond, and now it was too late. His brother was dead, and there wasn't a thing he could do to bring him back. There was nothing he could say and no amount he could pay to fix this, and the mere thought of these realities was devastating.

Then, if that wasn't enough, Derrek also couldn't stop thinking about the cruel thoughts he'd had just before listening to Dixon's voicemail. He'd been thinking how when he got out of the shower, he would finally call Dixon back to set him straight once and for all, so he'd never have to hear from him again. This, of course, bothered Derrek more than anything because in a matter of hours, Dixon had passed away, Derrek's wish had come true, and his angry words would haunt him forever. Worse, their own mother hadn't even attended her son's funeral, even though their father had found her and told her the day and time of it. It wasn't like Derrek had wanted to see his mother, anyway—or even his father again for that matter—but he still couldn't imagine any mother not wanting to see her son one last time before he was buried.

There was also something else, too, though, that broke Derrek's heart: the very candid, yet disturbing letter Dixon had written and left for him in a sealed envelope. Nina had given it to Derrek the day after Dixon's funeral, and now Derrek pulled it from his briefcase. He'd read it no less than twenty times, but he still couldn't believe what Dixon's life had been like over the last three years.

Derrek removed the two-page, handwritten letter from the envelope and unfolded it.

My dear brother,

If you're reading this letter, it means I've passed on, and while I'm hoping and praying we finally got a chance to talk and see each other before that happened, I still wanted to write this letter just in case we didn't. For the most part, I'm not even sure where to begin, so I'll just start by saying how terribly sorry I am for the way things turned out between us. I was dead wrong for the way I constantly abused your kindness over the years, and I am profusely sorry for not paying you back your money. What I did was uncalled for, and I hope you can somehow find it in your heart to forgive me.

The other thing I wanted to tell you was that these last three years of my life have been the worst. I went from finding out I had cancer, which Nina will tell you more about, to doing something you and I both swore we'd never do. I started using drugs. First I dabbled a little with marijuana, then I ended up trying a little cocaine, but it wasn't long before I moved on to smoking crack. To this day, I still don't know exactly why or how I resorted to all of this, except I think I'd finally come to a point where I simply couldn't take all the sad feelings anymore. After that last phone call you and I had, I couldn't eat or sleep, and I barely said more than a few words to anyone, including Nina. I was a total mess, and all I knew back then was that I needed something to take my mind off of everything. I wanted to forget about all my problems and all the regret I was feeling, and the next thing I knew I was using. I was caught up in a way like you could never imagine, and my addiction practically ruined both my life and Nina's.

Anyway, I guess the good news is that I finally agreed to get help, partly because Nina threatened to leave me, so I thank God for that. Of course, now that I have cancer again and my doctors have given me only a short time to live, I wish I hadn't wasted so much time getting high. I wish I'd found another way to deal with all the pain I was feeling, but now it's too late. The other thing I regret is not doing everything I could to help Mom and Dad. I know you and I made a pact many years ago to never have anything to do with either of them, but D, I have to tell you . . . if I had it to do over, I would spend my life trying to get them into treatment. I would do whatever I had to to help them because I now know firsthand what it feels like to want a fix so badly you'll do just about anything to get it. I know what it feels like to love crack so much that you don't care about anyone or anything around you. All you want is to feel better. You want your pain to go away by any means necessary, and you just can't seem to stop yourself.

Derrek didn't bother reading the last few lines of Dixon's letter because it was that particular part that Derrek wasn't too happy about. Dixon had made a request of Derrek, the kind of request he would never be able to honor, so he folded the letter back up and slipped it inside the envelope. Then he leaned back in his chair in tears. No matter how many times he read his brother's words, they were still pretty hard to digest. Even when Denise had finally told him about the conversation she'd had with Nina the night Dixon had died and how Dixon's drug use was the reason they had no money, Derrek still hadn't been able to figure it out. Not when Dixon knew full well what drugs could do to a person. Not when they'd both seen how severely crack had destroyed their parents.

On the other hand, though, Derrek understood completely why his brother had taken such a strong liking to all of the above: It was like he'd said, he'd wanted the pain to go away. He'd needed something to mask reality and fill his voids. Yes, Derrek, especially now, understood exactly what his brother had been going through and why he'd made the decisions he had.

Derrek sat for a few minutes longer and without warning, he burst into tears all over again. He covered his face with both hands, sobbing uncontrollably. He did this for what seemed like minutes but then he got up from his desk, strolled over to his door and locked it. When he returned to his seat, he opened his briefcase again and pulled out a plastic baggie of coke. He poured a bit of it on top of a black hospital three-ring binder and pulled out a razor blade to cut his line with. He much preferred using a mirror but since he didn't want to take a chance of having it shatter inside his briefcase, he never carried one around. It was okay, though, because he'd discovered that the binder worked just as well when he was at work, anyway.

He pulled out a rolled-up dollar bill, lowered it to the line of cocaine and snorted it. He leaned back, closed his eyes and within three or four minutes his high was in effect. He smiled even, because already he felt a hundred percent better. No pain, no worries, no tears, and life was good. He wished he could feel this way forever, but after another ten minutes passed, there was a knock at his door. Derrek's eyes sprang open, he sat up straight and hurried to put everything away. "Just a minute," he said, closing his briefcase and forcing it under his desk. Then he stood, wiped his nose as thoroughly as he could and went over and opened the door. His heart thumped madly when he saw John, the hospital CFO, standing before him with a strange look on his face.

"Please come in," Derrek said, trying to act as normal as possible.

John walked in and took a seat. "So how are things going?"

"Fine," Derrek told him but didn't like the look of suspicion on his boss's face.

"Well, the reason I wanted to talk to you is because you don't seem fine. You seem out of sorts and as much as I hate having to say this, your work is slipping."

Derrek's heart beat wildly. "I know, and I'm very sorry for that. I guess I'm still having a hard time dealing with the loss of my brother, but I promise you things are going to be different. Starting today."

"Maybe you need a little more time off."

"No, not at all. I'll be fine. I'm going to pull myself together and do what I have to do."

John acted as though he didn't believe a word he was saying. "You also don't look too well, Derrek. Are you maybe coming down with something? Your forehead is even sweating."

Over the last month, Derrek had noticed the sweating thing himself, and although he knew it was likely a symptom of his cocaine use, he said, "Yes, I think I might be getting a cold."

"Then, maybe you should take the rest of the week off."

"Well, if it's okay with you, I think I'll leave now but just for the rest of today. Once I get a full night's rest, I'll be good."

John stood up. "I hope so, and if you find that you need more time, just call me."

"I will, and thanks so much for understanding."

As soon as John left, Derrek sighed deeply; partly because he was relieved John was gone, but mostly because John had totally ruined his high. Derrek had been in such a good place emotionally before John had showed up at his door, so now he debated what he should do: snort another line right now or just wait until he got home, especially since no one would be there this early in the day.

He thought about his options a bit longer, weighing one against another, but then he made a decision.

"Home it is," he said.

Chapter 12

No matter how many years passed, no matter what they'd gone through, there was nothing that compared to lying in Derrek's arms. As it had turned out, Denise had found herself completely overwhelmed with work and for the first time in a while, she'd told Mr. Hunter she needed the afternoon off. She'd left the nursing home around eleven thirty and had arrived home by noon, and it wasn't until then that she'd learned Derrick had taken the rest of the day off, too. Now, they lay together, basking in the afterglow. They'd always heavily desired each other, but now it seemed as though they couldn't get enough. They had exceptionally strong urges to have sex all the time, so not only was the cocaine doing wonders for Derrek's depression, it was doing the same for their overall intimacy and Denise had no complaints. It was also helping her cope with all her work stress, along with her great desire to be the best director she could be. She was still overloaded and understaffed, but after Dixon's funeral, she'd made a conscious decision: she would do what she had to do to make things better. Sometimes she still took Vicodin and she'd even tried those Dilaudid pills Butch had given her, but neither compared to coke. They just didn't relax her in the same manner or provide the same intense euphoria.

Denise nestled closer to Derrek and exhaled. "I'm so glad we both decided to come home."

Derrek stroked her hair. "Me, too. And to be honest, I wish I never had to go back."

Denise wasn't sure she liked the sound of that, but she also knew Derrek was still in mourning and that it might be a while before he was his old self again. He was hurting, and she understood the reason he felt the way he did. "You'll feel better in time."

"I hope so. But on another note, we need to call Butch. We're running a little low."

"Yeah, I guess so," Denise agreed but thought about her pledge to stop doing drugs altogether, the one she'd made the day that police officer had pulled her over. She'd truly wanted to quit for good, but for now, drugs helped her and Derrek cope with Dixon's death.

She also knew Derrek was totally right about them needing more because not only had they gone through the cocaine supply she'd purchased the Friday Dixon had died, they'd also purchased another thousand dollars' worth three days later, along with another thousand's worth every week since then—and used most of that up, as well. Initially, they'd been able to cut ten to fifteen lines from a gram, but now they were lucky if they cut six or eight because they'd increased the size they snorted. They would never exceed spending a grand a week, though, so Denise wasn't worried.

Derrek lifted his cell phone from the nightstand and dialed Butch's number.

He answered right away.

"Hey, how's it goin'?" Derrek said.

Denise couldn't hear Butch's response but after he and Derrek made a bit of small talk, she heard Derrek saying, "I think we'll get a full twenty grams this time."

They'd never gotten so much in a single buy before, but actually Denise was sort of glad Derrek was purchasing as much as he was because this way, it would last them for two full weeks. It was easily going to cost about two thousand dollars, but that was okay.

Derrek and Butch exchanged a few more words and then Derrek told him he'd meet him in a couple of hours. When he laid his phone down, however, he sat on the side of the bed and pulled a square mirror from his drawer. Denise got to her knees on the bed, positioned herself behind her husband and hugged him around his neck. She hadn't thought about it before, but now she was glad Mackenzie didn't have debate practice today, which meant she could ride home with Alexis, and Denise wouldn't have to go back out to get her. This also gave her and Derrek more time to relax together.

Derrek cut four equal lines, snorted two of them and then passed the mirror to Denise. She sat down in the middle of the bed, picked up the dollar bill, and snorted the lines Derrek had left for her. They both moved their bodies toward the headboard, leaned back, and let the drug do what it did so well: send them to a whole other planet. They sat still for a while longer, but then Derrek slid farther down on the bed and pulled his wife on top of him.

"Baby, I love you so much."

Denise smiled at him. "I love you, too. I love you with everything in me."

Derrek gently grabbed both sides of her head and kissed her forcefully. Denise kissed him back, and she couldn't wait to make love to him again. Her high was in peak range, she was in bed with the man she loved to pieces, so what could be better?

The answer: not a single thing.

* * *

Derrek had just pulled out of the driveway, and Denise walked into the study on the first floor. She and Derrek had taken a shower together, but as they'd gotten dressed, she'd sort of been thinking about their monthly budget, something she'd always kept tabs on like a hawk. She still wasn't worried about anything, but she also wanted to see exactly where they were financially.

She clicked on the Internet Explorer icon, typed in the HTML address for their bank, and entered her user ID and password. She waited a few seconds, and before long, a balance summary displayed on the screen for their three accounts. Denise carefully scanned the totals and was soon a bit more at ease; mainly because even though they'd increased their monthly spending, they still had a pretty good nest egg. Five thousand in savings, three thousand in checking, and thirty-five thousand in their money market account. The other great thing was that she'd already paid bills for the month of October, so once she and Derrek got paid this Friday, they'd be depositing more than enough to cover the two thousand dollars Derrek would be withdrawing from checking this afternoon. He was on his way to the bank now to get the cash he needed for Butch.

The other plus was that while they had spent an extra four thousand over the last month, they'd still been able to save a little. Not nearly as much as they had every two weeks over the past five years, but something was better than nothing. She also knew this kind of spending wouldn't last forever. Sure, as of late, because of the pain Derrek was struggling with, they'd upped their cocaine usage a few notches, however, once things returned to normal, they would only use it socially the way they had in the beginning. Not to mention, knowing Derrek, it wouldn't be long anyway before he woke up some random morning with another huge epiphany: that he'd had enough and he was giving up drugs for good. When he did, Denise would give up everything, too, including pills, and that would be the end of it.

This would be all good news for their family as a whole because the last thing the two of them wanted was to become financially drained and jeopardize Mackenzie's future. Actually, they'd already saved around twenty thousand toward her college expenses, funds that were tucked away separately in a CD account at their credit union, and they were also hoping Mackenzie's glowing academic history would qualify her for scholarships. She earned As in every subject pretty regularly, and Denise didn't see where that would change once she was in high school.

Denise signed out of the online banking system, but just as she did, the home phone rang. She leaned over to see who it was, and smiled when she saw her mother's cell number.

"Hey, Mom."

"Hey, sweetie. How are you?"

"I'm good."

"And Derrek?"

"He's still not completely okay, but he's getting there."

"Glad to hear it. Also, I called you at work and they said you'd taken the afternoon off. Then, when I tried your cell and didn't get an answer I got a little worried."

"Everything's fine. Just needed some time at home is all."

"It's your job, isn't it? Honey, how long are you going to keep this up?"

"It's rough now, but it'll get better."

"Maybe you should look for another position. Maybe something at a smaller facility."

"That might work except I really love my boss and the nursing home as a whole. I just can't see myself going somewhere else."

"Well, I wish you'd at least think about it, because you seem so exhausted and stressed out all the time."

"It won't always be this way, Mom."

"I hope not. Also, how's my beautiful granddaughter?"

"She's good. She can't stop talking about our Christmas trip to Jamaica, but she's doing well."

"I wish your dad and I were going with you, but unfortunately, I have to work as closely as possible with the coordinator for the firm's Christmas party. It wouldn't be so bad, but of course, this year we're having it much later in the month than usual, and you guys will already be gone."

"I understand," Denise said but deep down all she could think was how this was the way things had always been with her parents, even when she'd been growing up. Her dad's career and business associates had always taken precedence over anything family related. She even remembered the time they'd missed a family funeral simply because her parents had planned a massive shindig at their home for all her father's partners, associates, and their spouses. Her mother hadn't wanted to miss her sister's funeral, but as always, her father had made it clear that business obligations and social appearances were priority. He'd told her mother that there wasn't a lot they could do for a dead person, anyway, and that it was better to be strong and to cherish her sister's memory.

"Maybe next year, though," Wilma added.

"Maybe so. It would be a lot of fun."

"Okay then sweetie, I won't hold you but please give my love to Derrek and Mackenzie."

"I will, Mom, and tell Daddy I said hello. Love you."

When Denise hung up the phone, she stood and went into the kitchen. She pulled the refrigerator open and while she saw a few leftovers, a package of string cheese, some cups of yogurt, juice, soda, cold cuts, and water, she suddenly felt restless and closed the door. She wasn't sure why, with all the rest she and Derrek had gotten this afternoon, but for some reason, she felt out of sorts. She didn't want to think it had anything to do with the conversation she'd just had with her mother, but in the back of her mind, she knew the thought of her "perfect" childhood tended to bother her much more than she was willing to admit. She guessed because it hadn't been perfect at all, and what no one else knew—except she and her parents—was that they had skeletons just like anyone else. They had secrets, and no matter how much Denise tried to forget about them she couldn't.

Denise casually walked back upstairs to the master bedroom and pulled out a couple of Vicodin, but then she dropped them back into the bottle and pulled the coke baggie from the box they kept it in. She knew she and Derrek had already snorted some twice this afternoon, but she still poured enough onto the mirror to make two more lines. When she separated the powder, she sniffed it into her nostrils one at a time and then lay across the bed, curled into a ball. She lay there, waiting for the fabulous feeling she knew it would give her, and it didn't disappoint.

She felt wonderful. So, she closed her eyes, took a deep breath, relishing every moment.

One Year Later

Chapter 13

Derrek dashed inside the elevator as fast as he could, pressed the button for the fifth floor at least eight times, and waited for the car to arrive on the floor his office was located on. He'd overslept yet again, and he was officially two hours late. "Come on," he said panicking and beating the button another couple of times, praying it would somehow force the elevator to move more rapidly. It didn't, of course, but soon the doors finally opened, and Derrek hurried down the hallway. He ignored any and everyone who spoke to him, quickly walked inside his office and shut the door. Thankfully, he hadn't run into his boss or anyone else who might have something to say about his tardiness, so maybe he was safe this time. He wasn't sure how this had happened again because he'd made it a point to set the alarm clock for five thirty. At least he thought he had. And he also remembered Denise coming into the bedroom telling him it was time to get up or he was going to be late. But somehow he must have gone back to sleep when she and Mackenzie had left. Either way, he was late, and it wasn't good because, as it was, John had already written him up a couple of times. There had been more than a few conversations about his attendance and tardiness issues, and John had also talked to him several times about his quality of work. Derrek knew things hadn't been right for a while, but he truly was trying to get his act together. He was doing all he could to get himself back on track in every area of his life, but maybe he wasn't trying hard enough.

But just as he attempted figuring things out, there was a knock at his door. At first, all he did was close his eyes, but then he willed his body out of his chair and moseyed over to see who it was. He had a feeling—a bad feeling—that it was John, and suddenly he felt faint. "Dear God please let it be someone else," he whispered. Derrek stood for a few more seconds without moving, and then he opened the door. Sadly, it was in fact John who was standing there.

"Derrek, I need to speak to you," he said, walking in and closing the door behind him.

Derrek had never been more nervous, and he'd also never seen such a stern look on John's face.

Derrek leaned against the edge of the desk. "Okay. What about?"

"I'm sorry to have to do this, but we've decided to let you go. Effective immediately."

"What? But why?"

"Look," John said, already losing his patience, "I've given you chance after chance to turn things around, Derrek, but you just can't seem to do it. As a matter of fact, you've gotten worse."

"I really apologize, John. I've been through a lot over this last year, ever since the loss of my brother, but now I know I need help."

"You really do, and I hope you get it. But this is your last day working here. We've done all we can, and I can't cover for you any longer."

"John, I know I have a problem, and I'll see a counselor. I'll even join that support group here at the hospital for people who've lost loved ones."

"Derrek, please . . . please don't make this any harder than it already is."

"But I'm really gonna get help this time. I'll do whatever I have to."

John shook his head. "Derrek, that's all fine and well, but you and I both know that the reason you've missed so much work is because of your drug use. I knew something was very wrong the first time I spoke to you a year ago. Remember when you'd first come back to work, and I noticed all the sweating you were doing?"

Derrek was speechless. He wanted to deny everything John was accusing him of, but no words he wanted to say would leave his mouth.

"The best thing you can do now," John continued, "is start packing your personal belongings."

Tears welled up in Derrek's eyes. "John, I'm begging you. If you'll please just give me a chance to show you how serious I am about fixing things."

"The decision has already been made, and security is waiting right outside your door with boxes. I'll also be staying while you gather everything together."

"I don't believe this. After all the time I've put into this hospital, you're going to escort me out like some criminal?"

"You're an illegal drug user, Derrek, and we simply can't take any chances. I'm sorry, but we have patients to worry about, and this is policy."

Derrek couldn't recall ever feeling more humiliated than he was right now. He was actually being fired from a six-figure management position, and security was going to usher him out of the building in front of everyone. The whole idea of it was ludicrous.

John opened the door and two security guards strutted in with boxes. They never made eye contact with Derrek, but he could tell they meant business, and that they wanted him to start packing without delay. They wanted him out as soon as possible.

Derrek hated what was happening to him, but in a split second he thought about something much worse than being fired. How was he going to break this kind of news to Denise? Tell her that he'd lost his job and that she would now have to take care of all of them? How would he ever find the courage to look his daughter in the face again?

Derrek tried gaining his composure but before long, his knees buckled and he dropped down in his chair. What in the world was he going to do? He literally had no idea, and while he would never say it out loud, he felt like dying. He'd felt the same way the night Dixon passed, but for some reason, today, his thoughts of killing himself were much more real. This time, he could actually see himself doing it.

Hours had passed and no matter how many lines of coke Derrek had done, he still didn't know how he would break the news to Denise. He was a nervous wreck, and he had a feeling that maybe he'd snorted just a little too much because his heart raced frantically. He also thought he'd heard voices but every time he'd gone to check downstairs, there had been no one in sight. He paced back and forth and back and forth again, and then looked out of the bedroom window when he thought he heard a car pulling up. Sure enough it was Denise and Mackenzie waiting for the garage to open. Now, Derrek paced even more, and he hoped he wasn't having a heart attack. His chest tightened, and he also had difficulty breathing, so he sat down in one of the chairs over in the sitting area. He tried to calm himself as best as he could, but within minutes, Denise strolled into the bedroom and smiled.

"Hi, honey."

Derrek burst into tears, and she closed the door.

"Oh my God, honey, what's wrong?"

Derrek grabbed hold of her. "Baby, I'm so, so sorry. I really messed up."

"Honey, you're scaring me. Please tell me what happened."

Derrek released her and took a couple of steps back. But he just couldn't make himself say the words.

"Baby, what is it? Why are you so upset?"

Derrek dropped to his knees and grabbed her around her waist. "I lost my job today. They fired me and then escorted me out."

"They what? What do you mean they fired you?"

"Baby, they let me go."

"But why?"

"Performance, attendance, tardiness, you name it."

"I don't understand," she said, pushing him away from her.

Derrek stayed on his knees but looked up at her. "I didn't wanna worry you, but I've had some problems over the last few months. I've been late, I've missed days, and I've missed a number of deadlines."

"Oh my God!" Denise hugged herself, drenched with anxiety. "Derrek, what in the world are we going to do?"

Derrek got to his feet and took both her hands. "Baby, I can fix this, okay? I promise you, I'll take care of things, so please don't worry."

"Don't worry?" she yelled. She never even usually raised her voice at him, so Derrek knew she was livid. "How can I *not* worry?"

"I know this seems like the worst thing ever, but I'll get another job. I'll do whatever I have to. You just have to trust me."

"Oh...my...God," she said again. "Dear Lord, what are we going to do?"

Derrek wanted to say something, anything to reassure her, but when he saw extreme panic in her eyes, he kept his mouth shut. He remained quiet because he knew they were in deep trouble— he knew this because Denise loved cocaine as much as he did, yet now they would have to figure out how to pay bills and support their drug habit on one income. Yes, they were definitely in deep, deep trouble for sure.

Chapter 14

As soon as Derrek left to go visit a friend, a guy who he'd said might be able to help him find another job, Denise hurried down to the study, turned on the computer, and signed into their bank system. She waited for their account information to appear, but she'd never felt more beside herself. Never felt so much fear. How could Derrek have let something like this happen? What was he thinking? And why had he been missing work? Denise didn't know whether to feel sorry for or be angry at him, but what she did know was that there was no way they'd be able to make it on just her salary. She earned a good one, but with all the bills they had, a thirty-five-hundred-dollar mortgage, two car payments that totaled nearly two thousand, utilities, cell phones, insurances, credit cards and more, there was just no way they'd be able to make this work.

Denise took a deep breath, but as she scrolled through their account summary, she panicked again. Their savings account had a balance of only seventy-six dollars and thirty-nine cents, and their checking account barely had enough to cover the checks she'd written a couple of days ago. Worse, they'd withdrawn so much money from their money market account to cover their cocaine expenses, the balance had dropped to zero and the account had been closed. Thirty-plus thousand dollars gone in just a year—gone and with nothing to show for it. She'd known things were pretty bad for them financially, but it wasn't until now that she realized just how awful they truly were. She guessed because as long as they both worked, even without any savings to fall back on, they earned more than enough to cover their monthly expenses and to even pay some of their drug costs.

Denise reached over and picked up a stack of envelopes, and as she sifted through them, she noticed that the mortgage would be due again in two days and that both vehicle payments would need to be taken care of by next week. Thankfully, they were both getting paid three days from now and would be able to cover everything, but this would also mean they wouldn't have anything left for groceries or miscellaneous spending. Thanks to that extravagant trip they'd taken to Jamaica last year and all the cash advances they'd gotten, all four of their major credit cards were fully maxed out. They'd been so strapped for cash, Denise had also borrowed from and zeroed out her 401(k) retirement account. She was already in the process of paying it back through payroll deduction, but all that meant was that they now had another debt they had to worry about.

Oh how Denise wished they hadn't taken that trip to Montego Bay or the trip they'd gone on this past summer to Florida. Actually, the only reason they'd done the latter was because ever since Mackenzie had been a toddler, Denise and Derrek had always taken her on a summer vacation, and they hadn't wanted to disappoint her this year, either. She'd been so looking forward to it, and while they'd both known they couldn't afford it, they hadn't been able to tell her no. Then while there, they'd also spent just over three thousand dollars for food, souvenirs, and clothing, and now Denise regretted it. The other thing she could no longer deny was the fact that she and Derrek had clearly spent way more money on drugs than they should have. They still weren't drug addicts, but she had to admit they did enjoy cocaine and that it had officially become a normal part of their daily lives. So much so, they sometimes found themselves spending six or seven thousand dollars a month on it, especially when they had coke parties with some of their new friends and it was their turn to host a gathering. They never did this while Mackenzie was home, of course, but whenever she spent the night with her friend Alexis, or spent the weekend with her grandparents, Denise and Derrek usually had company until the wee hours. They'd gotten to the point where they worked hard at their jobs during the weekdays, relaxed in their bedroom with a little cocaine every evening, and then partied on the weekends. As a matter of fact, their lives and social calendars had changed so drastically, Denise's parents now questioned why they hardly saw them. Even Denise's best friend, Michelle, had wanted to know if she'd said or done something to offend Denise, because they rarely talked on the phone, went shopping, or had lunch anymore. Things had changed a lot, and now Denise wondered what would likely happen from here.

Another ten minutes passed and just as Denise prepared to shut down her computer and head back up to her bedroom, Mackenzie walked into the study.

Denise tried pretending that all was well and smiled. "Hey, sweetie. Finished with your homework?"

"Yes, but where's Daddy?"

Denise didn't like the worried look on her daughter's face. "He went to visit a friend."

"So are we going to lose our house now?"

"Honey, no, and why would you think that?"

"Because Daddy was fired."

Denise stared at her.

"I'm sorry, Mom, but I couldn't help overhearing."

"We're going to be just fine. So don't you worry about anything."

"But why has he been missing so much work?"

Denise hated this because the last thing she wanted to do was lie to her daughter. She'd had to do that a lot lately whenever she wanted to get away to her bedroom to get high, but she didn't want to lie to her about this. "He just did."

"Is it because of the drugs?"

Denise swallowed hard, trying to stay calm. "Honey, what do you mean?"

"Mom, I'm not a baby. I'm thirteen now, and I know you and dad snort cocaine. I've known for a really long time."

Denise was too stunned to speak.

"I know you're going to be mad, but when you and Daddy started going to your room every single night and closing the door until morning, I knew something was going on. I knew something wasn't right, so one day I searched through your closet and I found the box you keep it in."

Tears filled Denise's eyes. "Sweetie, you really shouldn't have done that."

"I know, Mom, and I'm really sorry. But you guys were really starting to scare me. You don't even spend any real time with me anymore. We don't even have family night the way we used to."

Denise knew she had to make up another lie. "But honey, it's only because your dad and I have been working so many hours. We have a lot on our plates, but I promise it'll get better."

"But even when we went to Florida this summer, you guys left me in the hotel all by myself. You were gone until six in the morning."

Denise's heart dropped. She wished Mackenzie's words weren't true, but sadly, they were. Unfortunately, she and Derrek had in fact left their daughter all alone from early evening to early the next morning, and it was all because they'd ventured out to find a drug dealer to buy from. They hadn't planned on being gone for so long, but one thing had led to another and the next thing they'd known, the sun had started rising. They'd simply lost track of time, and there was no way Denise could explain it—other than lying again.

"I know, honey. We went out, found a party and got a little carried away. We stayed out a lot longer than we'd realized, and I'm very sorry for that."

Mackenzie stared at her mother, and Denise could tell she didn't believe one word of her story.

"Mom, I'm really scared. I mean, what if Daddy can't find another job? You're always saying that our mortgage is the biggest thing we have to pay every month, so what if we can't afford to pay that anymore?"

Denise pulled her daughter into her arms. "Look, sweetie. We really are going to be okay, so don't you worry. You hear me?"

"Yes. But, Mom, can I just tell you one more thing?"

"Of course."

Mackenzie released her mom and looked at her. "You can always use my college fund if you have to, though, right?"

Denise forced a smile onto her face. "Honey, thank you for offering, but we would never do that. We've been saving that money for your education and that's the only thing we'll ever use it for. Okay?"

"I know, Mom, but I'm just saying this because... well, just in case you ever need it."

"Like I told you before, everything is going to be fine."

Mackenzie didn't say much else and while Denise had tried her best to convince her daughter that nothing was wrong, she knew their financial situation was a disaster. If Derrek didn't find another job very soon, things would become extremely difficult for each of them. So all she could hope was that the friend he was visiting tonight could help him find something new immediately. Derrek needed another job like yesterday, and that was an understatement.

Chapter 15

Derrek eased down onto the plush sofa. "Man, this must be the worst day of my life. I mean, can you believe I was actually fired?"

"No. I really can't," Warren said, sitting down next to him but leaving ample space between them. Derrek had told Denise he was going to visit a friend he knew who worked at a large corporation downtown, but in reality, no such friend existed. He hadn't wanted to lie to her, but with all the pressure he was under, along with the way she'd looked at him and yelled at him, he'd simply had to get out of there. He'd needed to get away, and the only place he could think to go was over to Warren's. Warren had been his closest friend at work—the friend who had given him his first hit of cocaine nearly two years ago.

"I just didn't see it coming. Not in my wildest imagination did I ever think John would let me go."

"None of us did. But man, can I be honest?"

"Go ahead."

"Your work had really started to slip, and you were calling in sick a lot."

"Still," he said, "I didn't think John would do this to me. Not with all the time and effort I put into that job."

Warren leaned forward and flipped on the television. "I'll be right back."

Derrek tried making himself more comfortable and also relaxing his mind but with all the madness twirling through his head, it was basically impossible. *Fired.* He'd really been canned from a position that paid him just over a hundred thousand dollars a year. The whole idea of it made Derrek cringe, and he knew he had to find another job ASAP. The only thing was, though, he definitely wasn't stupid, and he knew it would be a while before he could even pass a drug test. If only he could find a position at a company that didn't require one. But he knew that would never happen, especially when it came to the kinds of high-paying jobs he'd be applying for. Boy, had he messed up big time, and he had no idea what he was going to do about it. He'd told Denise he was going to fix things, but truth was, he'd never been more clueless.

Warren came back into the room with a clear bag that held something white in it, but it didn't look like powder. As he moved closer and sat back down on the sofa, Derrek knew why. It was crack, and Warren had brought a clear glass pipe back with him, as well.

Derrek raised his eyebrows. "Wow, so it's like that?"

"Yeah, man. Haven't done powder in a little while now. I mean, I do it whenever I'm hangin' at your house, but only because that's all you have. But other than that, it's rock all the way for me."

Derrek wasn't sure how to feel about that. He knew the fact that he and Denise were snorting coke was bad enough, but for some reason he'd always shied away from crack. It seemed more streetlike to him and a bit too hardcore, and to be honest, he was a little afraid of it.

Apparently, Warren sensed what he was thinking because he

looked at him and said, "Don't knock it until you've tried it. I was just like you, but now my motto is this: 'Once you try crack you never go back.' Instead of waiting three to four minutes to get a full buzz like you have to with that powder, this right here will have you high as a kite in seconds. And the feeling is much more intense."

Derrek gazed over at Warren's crack supply and paraphernalia and while it all sounded very tempting, he was still pretty hesitant. He wasn't sure why, but something told him that doing crack was going too far. As it was, he and Denise had already gone further than they'd ever planned with regular cocaine and ended up with dire results.

Warren cast his eyes at him and then pulled out one of the dingy, yellow-white rocks, dropped it inside the round part of the clear glass pipe, and flicked a lighter. He held the fire just below the pipe, directly under where the rock was sitting, placed his lips around the skinny tubelike section sticking out from it, and inhaled multiple times. Derrek watched with great curiosity, and Warren passed it over to him. Derrek desperately wanted to say no, but since Warren had already leaned his head back in total silence, Derrek knew better than to ruin another man's high. He could tell Warren was floating in crack heaven, and that he was feeling fabulous.

Why was this happening? Why after all that Derrek knew about his parents and their horrible addiction, not to mention what he'd learned about his brother's excessive drug use, was he even considering something like this? Why was he doing this to himself? Why did he feel this great need to get high, and more so, why couldn't he seem to get a handle on it when he knew how wrong it was? Why couldn't he just stop all the madness and do what was right?

Derrek sat, debating his choices, but he finally set the pipe and the lighter on the glass coffee table. Then he picked both items back up—and set them back down again. He fought the urge to light the alluring rock with all his might, but the more he thought about the loss of his job, the distraught look he'd seen earlier on Denise's face, the possibility of maybe not finding another job as quickly as he needed to, along with the death of his brother, he soon gave in. He needed the pain and frustration of his realities to go away. He needed to forget about everything. He just wanted to feel better, so he picked the pipe and lighter back up and smoked his first dose of crack. He inhaled deeply and within seconds, his pain, problems, and worries disappeared. To him, they'd never even existed, and he wished he could feel this way forever. It was the reason he smoked another rock a half hour later—something he hadn't been able to stop himself from doing once he realized his high was practically gone already. It hadn't lasted very long at all, seemingly not more than twenty minutes, but thankfully Warren had a fairly full bag, and he was more than willing to share it. Derrek wouldn't make smoking crack a habit, but for now, this little white rock gave him what he needed, and he was grateful for it. He was very grateful for Warren's generosity indeed.

Chapter 16

Denise clicked on her nightstand lamp, sat straight up in bed and stared at her husband like he was crazy. "Derrek, where in the world have you been?"

Denise noticed that he could barely look at her and how it had taken him just a wee too long to answer her question. "Baby, I don't know what happened. I stopped by Warren's and the next thing I knew, I'd fallen asleep."

"Warren's?" she yelled. "What were you doing over there?" She already had a pretty good idea, but she still wanted to hear him say it.

"I just went to visit him."

"Until almost five in the morning? That sure was a whole lot of visiting for two men to be doing. And what about that friend you told me you were going to see?"

"I went there first, but after that I dropped over to Warren's, we had a little too much to drink and I guess I passed out."

"Yeah, right," she said, getting up. "And anyway, Derrek, who is this so-called friend of yours that works downtown, anyway?"

Over the last few hours, Denise had taken some time to think, and that's when it had dawned on her that Derrek had never once told her this friend's name.

"Leonard Weaver."

"Really? Funny how you've never mentioned him before."

"I met him through Warren a long time ago. He watches games with us sometimes."

"This is crazy. Sixteen years of marriage and now you're suddenly staying out all night? Did you need to get high that badly?"

"Baby, that's not why I went over there. I just wanted to talk to Warren."

"You're such a lying bastard."

Derrek squinted his eyes. "Baby, where is all this coming from? Why are you so upset? I made a mistake, and I'm sorry."

Denise rolled her eyes in disgust and brushed past him, almost forcing him into the dresser. She kept going, though, without looking back and as soon as she entered the bathroom, she slammed the door. She wondered what was wrong with her because it was so unlike her to blow up at anyone, let alone Derrek. She certainly had never called him a bastard before. There was no doubt that she had every right to be angry with him for staying out so late, but she still couldn't explain her impromptu mood swings. She was outraged and completely irritated, and she wondered if it was because she'd snorted the last of their cocaine supply shortly after finishing her conversation with Mackenzie, when deep down she'd wanted more. She'd tried not to think about it and now that Derrek had lost his job and they had no savings to fall back on, she'd told herself a few hours ago she was done with coke for good. She'd made this decision because there was no denying their cocaine use was the cause of all their problems, but what had grabbed her attention more were her daughter's words. Her sweet, kind, and considerate little Mackenzie had actually suggested they take her entire college fund to pay the bills. Denise had tried to keep her composure as much as she could, but as soon as Mackenzie had gone back upstairs, Denise had cried a puddle of tears. Her daughter's gesture, along with the troubled look in her eyes, had torn Denise apart, and she hated what all of this was doing to her. Mackenzie had just turned thirteen a couple of months ago, yet here she was worrying about household finances the way adults did.

Denise stared into the mirror over her vanity, seeing how exhausted she looked, and felt her hands shaking. Her nerves danced all over the place, and now she wished she could have just one or two more lines of cocaine. For the first time ever, she truly felt like she needed it. But maybe that was only because this was the first time in a long time she didn't have access to any. For months, she and Derrek had made sure to never run out completely, so this was different. There was no coke in the house—not a single speck of it—and Denise felt more and more anxious by the second. Finally, when she couldn't take it anymore, she pulled a bottle of Vicodin from the lower right-hand drawer. She hadn't taken any of this in a while, but at the moment, anything would be better than nothing . . . and after all, these were nothing more than a couple of pain pills.

Denise filled a cup with water, tossed the pills into her mouth, and washed them down. She knew they wouldn't work as quickly as the coke did, so she strolled into the toilet area, shut the door, sat on top of the lid and waited. In the meantime, she picked up a copy of *Essence* magazine from the wicker basket in the corner and read a couple of articles. When she finished reading those, she picked up an old issue of *More* magazine and read some of those stories, too, and soon, a warm feeling eased through her body. She even closed her eyes and smiled about it.

But then to her great dismay, Derrek came into the bathroom and started talking to her. The door was still closed, but apparently he didn't care about that.

"Baby, how long are you going to be in there?"

"Why?"

"Because I need to use it, and because I want to talk to you."

"You do realize we have three other bathrooms, right?" Denise didn't want to speak to Derrek so coldly, but he was getting under her skin and she needed him to go away. All she wanted was to be left alone, so she could enjoy her amazing euphoria.

"Baby, I'm really sorry about everything. My job. Last night. Everything."

Denise wasn't sure what he wanted her to say, so she didn't say anything.

"Baby, are you listening to me? I'll get three jobs if I have to. I'll do whatever it takes to keep us afloat."

She still didn't say anything, and she sort of felt bad about the way she was treating him, but she couldn't help it. For whatever reason, she couldn't seem to shake her hot-tempered attitude.

Finally, after Derrek spoke a few more words, he walked away.

Denise leaned back and relaxed against the tank, closed her eyes and folded her arms. How had their lives turned into such disarray? How had it changed so drastically in such a very short period of time? Yes, she knew drugs had played a major role in how they'd arrived where they were currently, but it still didn't seem real.

Not one time since meeting Derrek had she ever felt such scorn and lack of respect for him, but she knew part of her anger was much bigger than that. She knew much of her fury was geared toward herself for ever trying cocaine, and she also worried about what her father would say if he somehow found out about it. He'd be completely incensed if he knew Derrek was unemployed, and worse, Denise and Derrek had both spent thousands of dollars on drugs over the last twelve months. No matter how many times Denise played the whole scenario in her head, she still couldn't fathom it. She knew the money was gone, but she kept hoping that at some point in time she'd wake up from a torturous nightmare and that would be the end of it. That way her parents, especially her father, wouldn't have to find out about anything. It went without saying that she was a full-grown woman, but after all these years, she still felt obligated when it came to making her father proud. She felt this great need to uphold their family's reputation in the community and if any of her parents' friends or her father's colleagues ever got wind of Denise and Derrek's troubles, her father would never forgive her. He loved Denise, but he expected perfection with everything, including the way his daughter and son-in-law lived their lives, and he would never understand or tolerate something like drug use or *his* son-in-law being fired. To him everything was about decorum, restraint, and good manners, no matter how impossible that might be to portray sometimes, and it wouldn't be beyond him to disown them if they forced him.

Denise was glad the Vicodin had finally taken effect because she couldn't imagine having to think about her father any longer without it. She also prayed those two pills she'd taken would get her through the next few hours, but truthfully, she knew she would likely need something more—more Vicodin...or more cocaine.

Chapter 17

Derrek sat in his Escalade, debating whether he should go inside the building he was parked in front of. On the one hand, he knew it might be best to figure out another way, but on the other, he really needed to make a purchase from Butch, and since Denise had confirmed that there was no money available in either of their bank accounts, he didn't see how he had any other choice: he had to use Mackenzie's college CD. He felt bad even thinking about it, but the more he continued weighing things back and forth, something struck him. If he played his cards right, he could walk away with not only enough money to pay Butch, but he'd also make enough money to add to Mackenzie's twenty thousand dollars instead of deducting from it. There was no guarantee, but he also knew the plan he had in mind was worth taking a chance on.

Derrek got out of his vehicle, set the alarm and headed toward the front entrance of the credit union. It was still early, so thankfully, not many customers were inside when he walked in. He looked over at the teller line but then saw a couple of customer service representatives, sitting inside separate cubicles. He walked over to the receptionist.

"Good morning, how can I help you?" a twenty-something young woman asked.

"Uh, I'd like to withdraw a CD we have deposited with you."

"Sure. Megan should be able to help you with that. Please have a seat."

The young woman picked up the phone and dialed Megan, and Megan immediately walked out and greeted Derrek.

"How are you today?" she said.

"I'm well."

"Please come in," she said, turning and walking back toward her work area.

Derrek followed her and sat down.

"So what can I do for you?"

"I need to withdraw a CD."

Megan placed her fingers on the keyboard of her computer. "Do you have the account number?"

"No, I don't."

"Name?"

"Derrek Shaw."

Megan typed in the information and clicked through a couple of different screens. "Derrek and Denise Shaw, address 5562 Winter Brook Lane?"

"Yes, that's it."

"And for security purposes, I'll need your date of birth and Social Security number."

Derrek recited the information, and wished the woman would hurry up. For some reason, it was starting to feel very hot in this place.

"Thank you. The account is owned by both you and Mrs. Shaw, but it looks like only one signature is required for withdrawals."

Derrek was relieved. He'd been pretty sure this was the case, but it felt good knowing there was nothing to stop him from getting the cash he needed.

"I do see, though, that this is a five-year CD, and since you still have two more years before it matures, you'll have to pay a penalty for early withdrawal."

"I understand."

Megan clicked on a few more items. "It looks like you'll be forfeiting six months of interest."

"That's fine."

Megan clicked to another screen, and Derrek wished she'd move on with it. He was so hot now, he was sweating.

"So will you be needing a cashier's check or would you like to place this in your savings account?"

Derrek had forgotten about the small account they had there. They'd opened it when they'd gotten the CD, but if he wasn't mistaken they'd never added to the initial one hundred dollars they'd deposited in it. "I'd like a thousand dollars in cash, and yes, the rest can go to savings."

"Not a problem. I'll get this taken care of as quickly as possible."

"Good," Derrek said to himself.

While Megan printed out the appropriate documents and did whatever else was required, Derrek thought about Denise and how upset she'd been this morning. She'd eyeballed him like she hated him, and acted as though he were the enemy. Derrek was still pretty shocked about that because no matter what had happened in their lives over the years, their love for each other had never changed, and they had one of the most stable marriages he knew of. Yes, he'd stayed out way too late and he was sure she'd been worried to death about him, but he'd be lying if he said he wasn't a little bothered by the fact that Denise had obviously forgotten the vows they'd taken. She was overlooking her agreement to stand by him and love him for better or worse, and Derrek wasn't too happy about that. As far as he was concerned, they were in this thing together, and whether he had a job or not shouldn't have made a difference.

Megan passed a few documents to Derrek. "If you'll verify all the information on each form and sign and date at all of the Xs, we'll be all set. Oh, and please sign the savings account withdrawal slip as well. I'm going to deposit the entire balance and then withdraw the money you want to take with you."

Derrek leaned forward, skimmed each sheet, wrote his signature and date multiple times and passed everything back to her.

"If you'll excuse me, I'll walk over to the teller station right now to get your cash."

"Thank you."

Megan went on her way, and returned in only a few minutes. She counted ten one-hundred-dollar bills, folded Derrek's document copies from the CD withdrawal, and placed everything in an envelope. "Is there anything else I can help you with?"

"No, I think that's it," he said, placing the envelope of money inside his black leather jacket. "And thanks for all your help."

"It was my pleasure."

Derrek got up. "Thanks again."

When he made it back out to the parking lot, he climbed inside his vehicle and turned the ignition. He'd left his cell phone lying on the seat, but when he picked it up he saw that he'd missed a couple of calls, both from Denise. She hadn't left any messages, so he decided it was better to call her back after he took care of business.

He drove out of the credit union's parking lot, headed two blocks down the street and turned into a gas station. When he got out and walked inside, he waited for the man in front of him to finish paying for the gas he'd pumped, and then the silver-haired man behind the counter smiled at him. "Can I help you?"

Derrek prayed he was doing the right thing. "Uh, yes. I'd like to get ten thirty-dollar scratch-off tickets."

The man hesitated and looked a little surprised. "Did you say ten?"

"Yes."

The man pulled ten tickets from the roll and scanned them. "That'll be three hundred dollars."

Derrek removed three bills from his jacket and slipped them into the slot under the security window. The sales clerk took them and passed the tickets over to him. Then Derrek walked off to the side, pulled a quarter from his jean pocket and scratched immediately. He scratched and scratched and scratched the silver squares off the first ticket until he'd revealed every one of them, but he'd won nothing. He did the same with the second, third and fourth tickets, but still nothing again. At this point, old memories resurfaced, and his heart raced a mile a minute. A few years ago, he'd become interested in the Illinois State Lottery, and what had initially started out as a small habit had eventually turned into a big one. In the beginning, he'd purchased several one- and two-dollar tickets every now and then, but soon he'd begun spending five to ten dollars on the lottery every single day. This had gone on for a couple of months, however, it was after that particular point that he'd moved on to five-, ten-, and twenty-dollar tickets and then ultimately thirty-dollar tickets. Over a two-year period, he'd won a few thousand dollars, but the only problem was, he'd always played just about every dime of it back and had ended up with . . . nothing.

But not today. No, today, he would win at least a couple thousand dollars, so he could return the thousand he'd gotten from the credit union back into the savings account and then he'd have another thousand to pay Butch with and also buy anything else he needed. All he had to do was scratch maybe another two or three tickets, and that would be it.

Derrek scratched more silver squares, but when he scratched the ninth ticket, he smiled like a Cheshire cat. *I knew it!* He'd won a hundred dollars. That wasn't the full amount he needed, but it was something. Next, he scratched his tenth and final scratch-off, but sadly, it was another bust the same as the first eight had been. Derrek wondered if maybe he should cut his losses and leave now, but he had a feeling that if he kept at it, he'd be glad he had. So he went back up to the window and purchased ten more thirty-dollar tickets.

However, with the exception of a few free tickets and fifty dollars, all the others had been losers. Of course, he'd already scratched the free tickets, too, and used the fifty dollars to buy another thirty-dollar ticket and one twenty-dollar ticket, and those had let him down, as well.

It just didn't make any sense. He'd lost six hundred dollars of Mackenzie's college fund, yet he still hadn't won anything. He really needed this to work because if it didn't, he'd have to go back to the credit union again, and he didn't want to do that.

Derrek went back over to the sales clerk and took his chances. "I'll have ten thirty-dollar and five twenty-dollar tickets."

This time the man shook his head, and Derrek was ashamed. But he had no choice and had to do what he had to do.

Once again, he scratched and scratched and scratched to no avail, but then, finally, he won five hundred dollars on his last twenty-dollar ticket. The grim expression on his face softened— until he realized that five hundred dollars wasn't enough. He needed a thousand to replace the money he'd taken from Mackenzie's account and a thousand to pay Butch. So what was a measly five hundred dollars going to do for him? Maybe if he kept his faith strong and bought another two or three tickets, that would do the trick. Yes, that's what he would do—and he did. Except once again, he couldn't stop, and the next thing he knew, he was flat broke. The entire one thousand dollars, along with the money he'd won while playing, had vanished and he was sick to his stomach. He felt queasy and he was light-headed and depressed, so he hurried out of the gas station and sat inside his SUV.

Dear God what have I done? Derrek wasn't sure what to think, and he certainly didn't know what to say, not even to himself. If only he could have won the money he'd come there for, his problems would have been solved—at least in the meantime, anyway. Now, though, he had no choice except returning to the credit union. He didn't want to, but it was his only viable option.

But first Derrek picked up his phone, ignored another call he saw from Denise and dialed Butch.

"What's up?" Butch said when he answered.

"Don't even ask. But hey, can you meet me?"

"I'm tied up for the next hour, but I can meet you after that. Your normal two grams?"

"No, a couple of bags of rocks."

"Whoaaaa. When did you start hittin' those?"

"Last night."

Derrek thought about the crack he'd smoked over at Warren's and how quickly his high had worn off. The other thing he'd noticed, too, was how the second rock hadn't seemed to get him as high as the first. He wasn't sure why but all he knew was that he would give just about anything to reach that first crack high he'd experienced just one more time. Subconsciously, he'd been reliving those particular moments and dwelling on how good he'd felt, but now he was slowly slipping into an uncomfortable state of depression. The money he'd lost inside the gas station had made him feel bad enough, but the depression he felt now was much worse, and he had to fix it.

"Rocks?" Butch asked him. "Are you sure?"

"Positive."

"How much?"

"Three or four hundred dollars' worth. And can you sell me a pipe?"

"Not a problem. I'll bring it with me, and it's on the house."

"Oh and just so you know, this is between you and me. No need to mention this to my wife."

"Of course. See ya soon."

Derrek hung up, drove out of the parking lot, and turned in the direction of the credit union. This really would be the last time he went there to withdraw any of Mackenzie's money.

It truly would be.

He promised.

Chapter 18

Some things never changed. Denise stood next to her boss, Mr. Hunter, listening to Agatha Bowman rant about absolutely nothing. Here a whole year had passed since the woman had become a resident there, and still she wasn't happy about anything. Let her tell it, everyone who worked at Prescott Manor was a bona fide idiot who never should have been hired in the first place. Agatha complained day and night, and she was so rude to the nursing staff no one wanted to take care of her. Most dreaded even going into her room.

Mr. Hunter tried to reason with her. "I'm very sorry about the noise."

"It's a pitiful shame for someone to pay as much as I do, only to have some senile old woman screaming at the top of her lungs. She does it all the time, and I'm sick of it."

Agatha was referring to a sweet little woman named Mary who everyone loved. Mary did have a bit of a memory problem, and she did sometimes yell out loud for no reason, but it certainly wasn't all the time or nearly to the extent Agatha was claiming. This woman was truly getting under Denise's skin, and Denise was becoming more and more irritated.

"Again, I'm very sorry," Mr. Hunter said, "and we'll see if

we can maybe get Mary moved down to the other end of the hallway."

Agatha glared at him over her reading glasses. "Another floor would be much better."

"I'm not sure we can do that because each floor is designed to accommodate certain residents with certain needs and illnesses."

"Well, do what you want, but if I still hear that woman after you move her, I won't be happy." Agatha spoke matter-of-factly, and Denise could tell she was basically threatening Mr. Hunter again. She did this often, and Denise wanted to tell her a thing or two.

"Is there anything else we can help you with?" Mr. Hunter asked, clearly at a loss for words.

"You can get a stronger backbone. Run a tighter ship. Do your job the way it's supposed to be done."

Mr. Hunter kept a straight face, and Denise wondered how he could do that. Because at this point, had it been her…

"And then there's *that* one," Agatha continued. "The one standing right next to you. She needs to get a better handle on her nurses and do some real work for a change."

Denise took a deep breath and bit her lip, and Mr. Hunter moved slightly in front of her. That witch. How dare she speak to them this way? Sure, Agatha had a ton of money and was a member of Covington Park's social elite, but she had no right treating people like trash. As it was, Agatha tended to work Denise's nerves almost daily, but today was much different and there was only so much Denise was willing to take—today Agatha was a lot less tolerable because Denise had left her Vicodin bottle at home and then realized the bottle she sometimes kept locked in her desk drawer was empty. When she'd discovered this, she'd nearly cried because the two pills she'd taken shortly after Derrek had slithered home hadn't done much of anything. Her good feeling had come and gone in a matter of minutes, and now she needed something else. She also couldn't stop thinking about cocaine and how if she could only buy one more bag, she'd be through with it for good. All she needed was just a little more to help her deal with work, their financial situation, and Derrek's job dilemma. After that, she would turn over a new leaf and never do drugs again.

Mr. Hunter tried defending her. "Denise is a wonderful employee who does over and above what is required of her, so I'm sorry you feel that way."

Agatha pursed her lips and raised her eyebrows. "Hmmph. Is that right? Well, I guess that's true if you call using drugs doing over and above what's expected."

A chill plunged through Denise's body. Why was Agatha saying something like this? Denise was so on edge she felt like exploding.

"Cat got your tongue?" Agatha said to Denise.

That was it. "Look, old woman, I don't know who you think you are, but I've had it with you! Not one person who works here wants anything to do with you, so why don't you go somewhere else? Or better yet, why don't you drop dead!"

Mr. Hunter jerked his head toward her. "Denise!"

"I'm sorry, but this woman is nothing but a troublemaker, and now she's gone as far as lying on me?"

"Pretend all you want." Agatha spoke nonchalantly. "But trust me when I tell you . . . I know a drug addict when I see one. My sister was addicted to painkillers, sleeping pills, and cocaine for years, so I certainly know the symptoms."

"What symptoms?" Denise screamed.

"Oh, you walk around here acting as though everything is fine, but it's only because you're one of the lucky ones. You're the kind of addict who can talk a good game, do what you need to do, and get away with it. You're what they call a functioning drug addict, but you're an addict nonetheless."

Denise's heart pounded, and she wanted to strangle this woman. Dear God, how did she know and why was she doing this to her?

Denise turned and walked toward the doorway. "I'm out of here, Mr. Hunter. This woman has completely lost her mind. Crazy witch."

Denise stormed away from the room, zoomed past several staff members, and a couple that was probably there to see a resident, and headed for the elevator. Thankfully, it opened as soon as she pressed the button, and when she arrived at her floor, she got off and walked straight to her office. When she shut the door, she sat down at her desk.

"Gosh," she said, already regretting her words to Agatha, even though Agatha certainly deserved to hear them. Denise could only imagine what Mr. Hunter must have been thinking, and she knew it wouldn't be long before he paid her a visit. If she could take her words back, she would, but it was much too late for that. But why had Agatha gone as far as making such damaging accusations? Sadly, they were true, but how had she'd known? What had Denise done to give herself away? Because not even Mr. Hunter had pulled her aside to question her work, nor had he suspected she was taking anything. She was good at her job, and unlike Derrek, she never missed any days. She was on time, and she got along with all the women and men who worked for her.

Now, Denise *desperately* needed her Vicodin. She was in an uproar, and without even realizing it, she tore through her drawers, looking for some like a madwoman. Yes, she'd already searched earlier that morning, but she was hoping she'd somehow overlooked it. She prayed she could find at least one or two, but she couldn't.

Then it came to her. Lula's doctor had prescribed her some Vicodin about a month ago because of the leg pain she sometimes suffered with. She was still one of Denise's favorite residents and no matter how long she'd resided at their facility, she still never made any waves, she still never complained even when maybe she should have, and she loved everyone. Denise thought back to the day one year ago when Lula's vitals had dropped pretty low and they'd sent her over to the hospital. She'd been diagnosed with pneumonia and had ended up staying there for more than two weeks. At one point, her physician had wondered if she would make it, what with her being in her eighties, but she'd soon gotten better and been returned to the nursing home. Denise had been very happy to see her again, and now she needed a favor from Lula. She needed some of her medication, and there was only one way she could think to get it.

When Denise arrived back up on the second floor, she walked a few steps, turned the corner and saw Pamela standing in front of her pill cart. She was preparing to pass meds to a resident whose room was two doors down from Lula's.

"So how's it going?" Denise asked.

"Busy, but good."

"Have you even taken a break yet?"

Pamela chuckled. "Please, what's that?"

"I know the feeling, so why don't you take one now?"

"The other nurses are all tied up with their own residents."

"I know, but I can handle this. You only have what three or four more to go?"

"Pretty much. Are you sure?"

"Of course. Plus, it never hurts for me to get some hands-on experience, anyway."

"I owe you," Pamela said and then explained a few of the medication dosages and some that had recently been changed.

"Got it," Denise said. "Now go ahead."

"I'll be back in twenty minutes."

When Pamela was out of sight, Denise moved the cart farther down the hall and then parked it in front of Lula's room. She wasn't sure exactly when Pamela might return, so she wanted to make sure she saw Lula as soon as possible, and then she would pass meds to the others. Before she walked in, though, she found Lula's blood pressure medication and her Vicodin bottle. She took a deep breath, pulled herself together and finally entered.

Lula sat in her leather recliner and smiled when she saw Denise. "Well, this sure is a nice surprise. So they've even got the boss working on the floor today, huh?"

"Yeah, I guess so. How are you?"

"Can't complain. Doin' just fine for an old lady."

"So you're not feeling any pain right now?"

"Not really. Actually, it's not bad at all."

"Do you want a pill just in case?"

"Nooooo. Take too much of that stuff as it is. I think I can make it until tonight or tomorrow."

"Are you sure?"

"Yep."

"Okay, then, here's your amlodipine for your blood pressure." Denise passed her pill to her, along with a cup of water.

Lula placed the pill in her mouth and swallowed all the water.

Denise took the cup and tossed it into the trash can. Then she went into the bathroom to wash her hands—and also so she could open Lula's Vicodin bottle and take what she needed. She poured three of them into the palm of her hand, wrapped them in a paper towel and slipped them into her pants pocket. Then, she closed the bottle and walked back into the room.

"Okay, well, I'd better move on to the next person, but you let us know if you need anything."

"I will, and it's always good seeing you, sweetie. I'm always so proud when I see you running around here managing things. And you have a kind heart, too."

"Thank you for saying that, Lula. You know I feel the same about you. You're one of the nicest people I know."

"I'll see you later, honey."

"Take care, Lula."

And you have a kind heart, too. Denise wasn't so sure Lula or anyone else would continue thinking that if they knew what she'd just done. To be honest, she couldn't believe it herself. She'd stolen medication from a resident. Literally taken something that didn't belong to her, meaning she'd broken the law. But the thing was, she'd needed that Vicodin. Now more than ever, and she prayed God would forgive her.

Although, at the moment, she had to turn her focus to something else because as she rolled the cart toward the next room, Mr. Hunter walked up to her.

"Denise, I need to see you. Now."

Chapter 19

$\mathcal{M}$r. Hunter sat straight up in his chair behind his desk. "I'm not even sure where to begin."

Denise started right in. "Mr. Hunter, I really don't know what came over me, but I am so sorry for speaking to Agatha the way I did. It was extremely unprofessional, and it will never happen again."

"I know Agatha is a handful and that she's been nothing but trouble since the beginning, but I'm terribly disappointed in you. This isn't your normal way of handling things, Denise, so I'm a little shocked about your behavior."

Now, Denise wished she'd taken the three Vicodin while she'd been in Lula's bathroom, because not only were her nerves racing, she felt agitated and physically exhausted. She was a total mess, and she couldn't wait to flee Mr. Hunter's office.

"But I have to tell you," he continued, "right now I'm more concerned about Agatha's comments about you. She made some very serious accusations."

Denise's heart beat faster. She hated being confronted and in-terrogated this way, especially when Mr. Hunter knew what kind of person Agatha Bowman was. He knew she didn't like Denise or anyone else for that matter, so why would he even bother questioning her?

"I'm not sure why she said the things she said, but she's lying."

"But she sounded so sure about everything. I know she's a cruel woman, but she sounded pretty convincing."

Denise's frustration turned to outrage. "So you're going to believe that bitter old woman over me? The person who has worked her natural behind off for you? You're going to take the word of Agatha Bowman over mine? Wow!"

Mr. Hunter gazed at her, seemingly unmoved by her theatrics. "There's no need to get loud, and I guess it's time I level with you. It's not just Agatha's comments that have me worried. It's my own thoughts and observations. I was hoping that maybe I was mistaken, and that's why I hadn't said anything, but Denise, I've wondered for a while now if something was wrong. It's hard to explain because your performance here at work is still top-notch, but there are times when you seem distant or like you're overly happy. Then there are times when you seem tired and like you haven't had much sleep."

Denise wasn't sure what to say.

"I've felt this way for a while, and it wasn't until Agatha said what she said that I knew it was time I sit down with you."

"That woman is a liar," Denise said matter-of-factly. "She's never liked me, and now she's trying to get me fired."

"Maybe, but I just feel like something's wrong. I know it's not my business, but is everything okay at home?"

"Everything's fine," she lied. "And the only real problem I have is the stress from this job. It's worse than ever, but I'm handling it."

"But why has your stress gotten worse when we've been fully staffed for a long time now?"

"I still have a lot of responsibilities."

"Then, do we need to consider hiring an assistant director of nursing for days and then split up the number of nurses that report to you?"

"No, that's not what I'm saying. I'm fine with things just the way they are."

Mr. Hunter was quiet.

"And just for the record," Denise said. "I would never use drugs. Not for any reason."

"I hope that's true because after you stormed away from Agatha's room, she suggested I have you tested."

Denise tried swallowing the huge lump in her throat but couldn't. What in the world was she going to do if Mr. Hunter listened to that crazy woman? "So you're actually going to force me to do a drug screen? All because of Agatha and her lies?"

Mr. Hunter leaned back in his chair, seemingly sighing of frustration. "I really don't want to, Denise. Believe me I don't. But if I notice anything else out of the ordinary, I'll have no choice."

"Oh...my...God," she said, narrowing her eyes and trying to sound as innocent as possible. "You can't be serious?"

"I'm sorry but I'll have no choice except to do the right thing."

Denise stood up in a huff. "Is that all?"

Mr. Hunter looked at her and nodded.

She took that as a yes and left his office. She hurried down the hall, onto the elevator, and up to her office again. She immediately shut the door behind her and couldn't make it to her desk fast enough. When she did, she snatched the bottle of water sitting near a photo of her, Derrek, and Mackenzie, pulled the three Vicodin from her pocket and took them. She'd rarely taken three at a time in the past, but lately two just didn't seem to be cutting it. She also hadn't had a morsel of food to eat so far today, so she sat down, leaned back, crossed her legs, closed her eyes and did her usual—she waited.

She did think about Derrek, mostly because she'd called him a few times and he hadn't answered, but right now he was sort of the least of her worries. It wasn't as if his so-called friend in corporate America actually existed, anyway, and could get him a job, and that was the only reason she'd even bothered contacting him—that and also to ask him how soon he was going to start contacting headhunters and sending out résumés. There was no telling what he was up to, but regardless, she wasn't happy with him about staying out so late. Although, it was like she'd just been thinking, Derrek was pretty much the least of her worries, and she wasn't about to let her thoughts of him, Agatha, or Mr. Hunter ruin the rest of her day. Her Vicodin would be kicking in soon enough, and life would be good. She'd be as content as always.

Chapter 20

*B*utch hadn't been able to meet Derrek after all, so for the first time, Derrek was headed to Butch's house. Well, not to the one he lived in per se, but the one he regularly sold drugs out of. In the past, Derrek and Denise had always made it a point to only buy from Butch at a designated meeting place but never at any of his "places of business." They'd always thought it would be too risky and they also hadn't wanted to see or consort with any of Butch's "other" customers. They'd wanted to stay clear of that but since Butch had called Derrek back, saying there was no way he could meet him until sometime after five, Derrek had asked if he could come by and pick up his package. He hadn't wanted to wait another five hours to get what he needed, so Butch had given him the address and a few directions.

Derrek waited for the light to change and then drove through the intersection. After that, his phone rang, and it was Denise again. He almost didn't answer, but something told him it was better to talk to her now so he wouldn't have to do so after he left Butch's.

He pressed the Send button and placed the call on speaker. "Hey."

"So where in the world have you been, Derrek?"

"I had things to do, and why are you asking?"

"Because I wanna know."

"You sure didn't have much to say this morning, though, now did you?"

"I don't believe you. You're the one who was careless enough to get fired, yet you're the one with an attitude?"

Derrek squinted his eyes and shook his head. "Denise, what do you want? Why are you calling me?"

"To see how many headhunters you contacted today."

"Why are you harassing me about this? I just lost my job, and I need time to figure things out. Geez."

"So you didn't call any?"

"I called a couple," he told her, hoping his lie would satisfy her and stop her from badgering him.

"Which ones? What were their names? And what did they say?"

When the light turned green, Derrek continued on his way. "So what is this, some sort of police investigation? Are you the newest member of the FBI or somethin'?"

"Excuse me?"

Derrek didn't know what was wrong with him. He didn't want to talk to his wife so curtly or defensively, but he couldn't seem to control himself. He was confused because right now just hearing the sound of her voice annoyed him.

"I'm not sure what your problem is, Derrek," she said, "but we have some serious issues to deal with. We have no money, and I hope you know that every dime of that paycheck you're getting on Friday will need to be deposited for bills."

"I know that, Denise. I'm not a dummy, so stop treating me like I am one."

"What's wrong with you?"

"Nothing. So is that all?"

"No, not even close. For one, Mackenzie is worried out of her mind, and she even suggested that we use her college fund if we needed to. She overheard us talking, Derrek, but of course, I told her that would never happen."

Derrek pulled up to another red light and closed his eyes. How could he have done this to his own daughter? Not only had he already withdrawn a thousand dollars of her money and lost it on lottery tickets, but he'd withdrawn another thousand right after leaving the gas station and then gone back to the gas station again. He hadn't planned on it, but something in his gut had told him he should try his luck one more time, so he had. But he'd lost it all, and had then had to go back to withdraw more money, a whole other thousand dollars, and now Mackenzie's account was three thousand dollars less than it should have been.

"Hellooooo? Are you even there, Derrek?" Denise asked, clearly infuriated.

"I heard you."

"And just so you know, I've been sitting here thinking about something else, too."

"What?"

"If you don't find a job within the next couple of weeks, which seems pretty unlikely to me, you're going to have to borrow from your 401(k)."

Derrek was quiet again because his 401(k) account was the last thing he wanted to think about.

"Why aren't you saying anything? Because you certainly didn't have any problem with me borrowing from mine."

"I'll do whatever I have to."

"And what does that mean?"

"Just what I said."

"Wow, you're really full of it today, aren't you?"

Derrek sighed. "Look, Denise, I've got a lot on my mind, so why don't I just talk to you later?"

"What time will you be home?"

"Soon."

"In an hour, two hours, when?"

Derrek balled up his fist and hit the steering wheel. "You're still at work, anyway, so what difference does it make?"

"Well, for one thing, Mac has a yearbook meeting, and she needs to be picked up."

"Don't you usually handle that?"

"Yeah, but since you no longer have a job, I think picking up your daughter is the least you could do."

Derrek hated this. He loved Mackenzie and would do anything for her, but today he had plans. Today, he wanted to pick up his package, smoke a little of it and then go hang out at Warren's. Warren wouldn't be off until after five, though, so maybe he could still pick up Mackenzie, drop her at home and then head over to his friend's after that. "Okay, fine. I'll pick her up."

"She should be ready around four thirty."

"I'll be there," he said as cordially as he could.

"Bye, Derrek."

He opened his mouth to say good-bye, too, but Denise hung up.

Derrek was stunned over the conversation they'd just had, and he was still taken aback by the way she'd spoken to him at home this morning, but he knew it was all because of this whole losing-a-job thing that had come between them. It was as if they'd become enemies in a matter of hours, when for years they'd shared the love of a lifetime. She seemed irritated by him, and he felt the same way about her, but what he couldn't understand was how the loss of a job could cause so much animosity between a husband and wife. It didn't make a lot of sense to him.

When another twenty minutes passed, Derrek rolled into the driveway and parked directly behind Butch's truck, but he didn't get out. Instead he called Butch the way he'd asked him to, and

Butch walked out of the house, wearing a navy-blue down jacket. He continued around the SUV, opened the passenger door and got in.

He didn't hesitate, letting Derrek know how he felt, though. "Man, I gotta tell you, I'm a little shocked to hear about you smokin' crack."

Derrek peered straight ahead, refusing to look at him. "Why?"

"A well-educated professional like yourself? Just doesn't seem right. I mean, in my line of work I see it all, but I just don't see you as a crack kinda guy."

"Well, I'm very sorry to disappoint you! So do you have what I came for or not?"

Butch pulled off his sunglasses. "Okay, wait a minute. Let's get somethin' straight. I'm not the enemy. So don't go gettin' all huffy with me just because you're sittin' here fiendin' for your next fix."

Derrek raised both his hands. "Man, I apologize. I was way out of line." Derrek still didn't know what was wrong with him. His temper and patience were unusually short, and while he'd thought these feelings were geared only toward Denise, now he knew almost anyone could aggravate him.

"Just don't let it happen again," Butch said, pulling a brown bag from inside his coat and passing it over to Derrek.

"How much I owe you?"

"Four."

Derrek pulled the hundred-dollar bills from his wallet and gave them to him, and Butch opened the door and stepped out.

"I'm really sorry for what I said," Derrek tried to explain.

"Yeah, whatever."

Derrek watched as Butch went up the sidewalk and back into the house, but there was something Derrek couldn't stop thinking about: Butch's words to him, the ones about him being a fiend. The words bothered Derrek because he'd said something similar to his father the night they'd argued in the hospital parking lot. *You're nothing like me! You're a no-good, deadbeat drug addict who only cares about his next fix.*

Derrek replayed both Butch's words and his own words more than a few times, but then he realized he was *nothing* like his father. Although, if that were true, then why had Butch's description of Derrek cut him to the core? Why had he even been reminded of that night at the hospital?

But Derrek didn't have time for any of this. What he needed to do was find somewhere close so he could park, relax, and smoke his crack in peace. All he wanted was to enjoy himself for a little while, pick up his daughter, and then spend the rest of the evening at Warren's. He wanted to be free of all chaos and everyone who caused it, including Denise.

Chapter 21

Vicodin just wasn't enough anymore. Denise had certainly come to love it over the last couple of years, but no matter how much she wanted it to suffice, it just couldn't match her love for cocaine. It simply couldn't relax her the way it once had because even after taking three pills a few hours ago, all at one time, she'd barely even noticed it. It had felt as though she'd merely taken a couple of aspirin, and she knew it was because her body had developed a high tolerance for Vicodin. So what was she going to do? Her nerves were shot, she was overly exhausted, and as much as she didn't want to feel the way she did about Derrek, she almost despised him. Their relationship had changed drastically, and she'd noticed something else, too. Just like she no longer saw the need to call him honey or any other pet name, he no longer called her baby. They were Denise and Derrek and nothing more than that. She also wasn't too happy with Mr. Hunter, a man who she had looked up to and adored from the time she'd begun working for him. But today, however, everything had gone wrong. Agatha had accused her of using drugs, and not only had Mr. Hunter believed her, he'd let on how he'd already had his own suspicions about something being wrong with her as well.

It was because of all this that Denise was at her wits' end. She knew she didn't have any money to buy from Butch, but if she didn't get at least a little cocaine before the day was over, she wasn't sure how she would make it through the evening—or even the next morning. Maybe Butch would let her have some coke on credit and then she could pay him once her check was deposited. That would only be two days from now, and since she and Derrek were regular customers, she didn't see where Butch should have any problem with it. There was the option of borrowing money from Michelle, but since Denise had basically kept her distance from her best friend for such a long period of time now, she wasn't sure Michelle would take too kindly to her asking for money. There were also her parents who could certainly afford to loan her any amount she asked for, but she'd rather die than let her father know what kind of shape they were in. The other option was possibly cashing in Mackenzie's college CD, borrowing a little from it, and then replacing it once Derrek borrowed from his 401(k) account. But the thought of that gave her an uneasy feeling because she just couldn't see taking from her own child. If she did, it would be the lowest of lows, and she wasn't sure she could live with that.

So maybe trying to cut a deal with Butch was the only way to go. It was the reason she called him from her car.

"I'm not sure how to ask you this," she said when he answered. "But do you think you can do me a favor?"

"Depends on what it is."

"We're a little short on money this week, but if you can give me a couple of hundred dollars' worth, I can pay you on Friday."

"Well, I guess I'm a little confused because your husband was just by here earlier, and from what I could see, he still had a few hundred, even after he paid me."

Denise frowned. "Oh really?"

"Yeah, and the only reason I'm telling you is because he sort of pissed me off. He got all nasty with me because I told him I was shocked about him using crack."

Denise paused before speaking, not wanting to believe what she was hearing. "Crack?"

"Yep. Said he just started using it last night."

So that's what he'd been doing over at Warren's. Cocaine was one thing, but crack was something different, and she wondered what Derrek was thinking.

"I take it you didn't know about that," Butch said. "Although, he did tell me there was no need to mention anything about this."

"To me?"

"Yep."

"I guess I don't know what to say." Denise almost told Butch that Derrek had lost his job, and the only reason she didn't was because she didn't want him thinking she might not have the money to pay him back on Friday when both she and Derrek got paid, particularly since this would be Derrek's last check.

"I just thought you should know what was up with your husband, especially after he snapped on me the way he did. But you and I are good, though, and paying me on Friday is cool."

"Can you meet me at the usual spot in a half hour?"

"Make it an hour," he said.

"Thanks, Butch."

"No problem."

Denise set her phone down, and while she'd planned to drive away from the nursing home's parking lot as soon as she hung up, she needed a few minutes to think. Crack? Derrek was actually using street cocaine, and he hadn't said a word. Now, she wondered if maybe this was the reason he was speaking to her so sarcastically and cruelly. She hadn't been all that nice to him either because of how on edge she'd been lately, but this whole crack business of his would definitely explain Derrek's newfound behavior. She also wondered if he'd lied to Butch about having used crack for the first time the night before. Now, she questioned whether maybe he'd been using it all along and that this was the real reason he'd missed days from work, not done his job the way he was supposed to, and gotten fired.

Denise tossed a few more thoughts through her mind and then drove out of the parking lot. A few seconds later, her phone rang. She smiled when she saw Mackenzie's cell number.

"Hey, sweetie."

"Mom, where are you?"

"What do you mean?"

"I've been finished with the yearbook meeting for almost an hour."

"Your dad never showed?"

"No, was he supposed to pick me up?"

"Yes, I talked to him earlier, and he said he'd be there."

"Well, he's not. But maybe he just forgot."

Denise wished she could strangle Derrek. How was she going to meet Butch and pick up Mackenzie all at the same time?

"Honey, I have something I have to take care of, so let me call Mom to see if she can drop by and get you. Okay?"

"That's fine. Call me back."

Denise pressed the End button and dialed her mom. The phone rang and rang but then went to voicemail. Now Denise panicked. She knew her father was still at work, and even if he wasn't, he was likely already caught up in Chicago's rush-hour traffic. Maybe Michelle could go get Mackenzie, but again, since she hadn't been in contact with her, she just couldn't bring herself to ask her.

Denise tried to think of someone else, but finally her phone rang. Thank God, it was her mother.

"Mom?"

"Hey, I'm sorry I missed your call. I was at the pharmacy picking up a few items, and I didn't want to answer while I was in line."

"I was calling because Derrek and I are both a little tied up, and Mackenzie needs a ride from school. Can you swing by and pick her up for me?"

"Of course. I'm not that far away from her anyhow. I can be there in fifteen minutes."

"Thanks so much, Mom."

Denise called Mackenzie back.

"Sweetie, your granny is on her way."

"Okay, but have you talked to Dad? I just tried calling him, but he didn't answer."

"No, I haven't. I'll try to call him, too, though."

"Okay, Mom. See you at home."

"Bye, honey."

Denise immediately dialed Derrek, but there was no answer. At first, she wondered where he was, but she had a feeling he was somewhere hanging out, high as the sky. Crack. He was actually smoking the one thing they'd both agreed to never do under any circumstances, but apparently, Derrek had changed his mind about the pact they'd made.

There was something else that bothered her, too. Where on earth had he gotten the money to buy anything? Neither of them had that kind of cash, so how had he come across hundreds of dollars? Nothing was adding up, but Denise would make it her business to find out as soon as possible.

Chapter 22

Denise hit the button on the overhead console of her car, the one programmed to the garage, and waited for the door to roll up. Her mother was parked far to the side, and Denise had sort of suspected she might still be there when she got home. It was the reason Denise quickly pulled down the sun visor with the lighted mirror and did a nose check. After meeting Butch in their normal spot, she'd driven farther around the park to a more secluded area and snorted a couple of lines of cocaine. She'd instantly felt better and more like herself, and she was glad she'd made the decision to call him. She was thankful Butch had given her what she needed on credit.

Denise twitched her nose, sniffed a couple of times and pushed the visor back up. Then, she eased into the garage, got out, and went into the house. Mackenzie and her grandmother were sitting at the island eating pizza.

Denise strolled over to her mom, who had a weird look plastered across her face, and embraced her. "Thanks so much for picking up Mac."

"I was happy to do it. Always glad to spend time with my grandbaby."

Mackenzie smiled and hugged Denise. "So Mom, did you ever talk to Dad?"

"No, I didn't. He must be really busy."

"Honey," Wilma said to her granddaughter, "why don't you run upstairs to your room so I can speak to your mom?"

Mackenzie gazed at her grandmother in a fearful sort of way, and Denise didn't like it. Mackenzie eventually stood and left the room, but she didn't seem too happy about it.

"Have a seat," Wilma said.

Denise sat across from her mother, wondering what this was about.

"Honey, why didn't you tell me?"

"Tell you what?"

"That Derrek had lost his job."

Denise's body went numb. Why had Mackenzie done that? Why had she told her grandmother any of what was happening in their household?

"I guess I didn't know how to."

"But why?"

"I know how much Daddy expects of me and Derrek, so I just didn't want you to know. Plus, Derrek will be back working in no time."

"But why was he let go? Is the hospital downsizing?"

Denise didn't want to add her mother to the list of people she told lies to, but there was no way she was telling her Derrek had been fired. "Yes, they're cutting back in all the administrative departments, and Derrek was one of the first they laid off."

"After all the time he's put in there? How awful."

"I know. He was pretty upset by it, and so was I. But, Mom... I'm begging you, please don't tell Daddy about this."

"But what if he can help in some way? Your father has a lot of connections."

"I know, Mom, but I want us to figure this out on our own."

"But I just think—"

"Mom, please. Please don't say anything to him."

Wilma sighed. "If you insist. But I still think it's a mistake not to tell him."

"We're going to be fine. Derrek has a wonderful background, and I'm sure he'll find something very soon."

"I hope that's true because if he doesn't, what will you do for money? How will you pay your bills?"

Denise had been tearing her brain out all afternoon trying to figure out that very thing, but she would never let her mother know how worried she was. She certainly would never admit that her pension fund was gone and that they had no savings whatsoever at their bank. So she lied again.

"We'll manage, Mom. We'll do whatever we have to do, even if it means using our savings."

"Well, at least you have that to fall back on, and that makes me feel a whole lot better about things."

Denise reached across the table and grabbed her mother's hands. "Please don't worry about us."

"You're my baby, and I love all three of you, so I can't help it. But I'm going to trust and believe that everything will be okay."

Denise smiled, but deep down, she couldn't have been more troubled or worried because not only did they not have any cash, Derrek was now using crack, she had no idea where he was, and she'd purchased a bag of cocaine on credit. And sadly, her gut told her things would only get worse. It was practically inevitable.

"Derrek, where in the hell have you been?" Denise yelled as loudly as she could. "Do you realize it's six in the morning? I've been calling you for hours."

Tears flooded Derrek's face, but he dragged himself closer to Denise and slumped to his knees. "Baby, I'm so, so sorry. Oh God, I really messed up this time."

Derrek grabbed her around her waist and laid his head against her stomach. But Denise pushed him away from her because yesterday morning when he'd fallen to his knees, saying he'd "messed up," he'd dropped the bomb about being fired. She also wondered why he was back calling her baby again.

"Derrek, what are you talking about?"

"Baby, I didn't mean it," he sobbed. "But I couldn't stop. I tried, but I just couldn't."

"Stop what?"

"Gambling."

Denise scrunched her face. "Gambling? What kind of gambling?"

Derrek struggled and got up and brought his hands together in the praying position. "Baby, what I have to tell you...it's real bad."

Denise drew in a deep breath and covered her mouth. "Wait a minute. Where did you get money to gamble?"

Derrek burst into tears all over again. "From...from...the credit union."

"Oh no," Denise said, tears already streaming down both sides of her face. "No, Derrek...please tell me you didn't. Not Mackenzie's college money."

"I didn't mean it, baby. I swear."

"How much of it did you spend?"

Derrek pressed both his temples with his hands and held his head down.

"How much, Derrek?" she screamed.

"All of it."

Denise dropped down on the bed, thinking about that year

Derrek had become obsessed with the state lottery. "Oh no. Dear God, please don't let it be. Derrek, are you telling me you spent twenty thousand dollars on scratch-off tickets?"

Derrek walked over and kneeled down in front of her again. "No... I mean, yes, I did spend some of it on scratch-offs, and I bought a little dope from Butch, but that's not where most of it went."

Denise's patience was wearing thin. "Well then what happened to it, Derrek?"

"Warren and I went to the casino."

"The casino? Are you crazy?"

"I know, baby, and I'm sorry. I have a problem, and I know it. I need help."

"No, what you need is to get off of me," she shouted and shoved him away from her.

Derrek fell over.

Denise stood up. "I don't believe this. You actually withdrew the entire balance and took it with you?"

"No, I only took two thousand," he said, pulling himself up and sitting on the bed.

"Okay, then I guess I don't understand."

"That's because, baby... it's complicated."

"Then, I wish you'd explain it."

Tears rolled down Derrek's cheeks. "I only took two thousand, but when I lost it, Warren hooked me up with this loan shark."

"I should have known Warren had somethin' to do with this."

Derrek sniffled. "He introduced us and the next thing I knew, I kept playing those slots and then the blackjack tables and the money was gone."

"But I still don't get how you spent all of Mackenzie's money if you only took two thousand dollars with you. It doesn't make any sense."

"Baby, the only reason I was able to keep playing is because I kept borrowing money from D.C. He's the loan shark I just told you about."

"And this D.C. person just assumed you were good for it? The man just casually loaned you thousands of dollars not knowing if you could pay it back?"

"He knew because I showed him the credit union receipt. It had the balance on it."

Denise stared at him. She knew it was her husband she was looking at, but the man who was speaking to her was a total stranger. The man she was gazing at now was a complete fool who didn't have a brain in his head. How could he have done something like this? How could he steal Mackenzie's money and then throw it away on nothing?

"When is he expecting his money?" she asked. Not that this would change how much Derrek owed him, but a part of her was hoping they'd be able to make payments.

"First thing in the morning. He lives ninety miles away in some city called Mitchell, so he's going to spend the night at a hotel near the casino. He's meeting me at the credit union at nine."

"Wow, Derrek. Wow. And if you don't pay him?"

"Baby, that's not even an option. Warren said that D.C. isn't someone to be played with. There's even a rumor about him killing people over his money."

"So not only have you thrown away Mackenzie's money, you've put our lives in danger?"

"All I have to do is pay him, and it's over."

Denise tossed him a dirty look. "Yeah, you got that right, it is over. Between you and me."

"Baby, please don't say that. I made a huge mistake, but you have to take some of the blame, too. I've thought about that a lot, and now I realize that's why I was so angry at you today."

Denise widened her eyes with rage. *What?* "Take some of the blame? Why?"

"Because everything was fine until that night Dixon died and you gave me that cocaine. Before that, I was drug-free and had been going to my support group meetings religiously. But then you gave me that cocaine, and things have been downhill ever since."

Denise's face tightened. "Don't . . . you . . . dare . . . blame this on me, Derrek! You're the one who brought that crap into the house in the first place. I had never even touched cocaine until I found it hidden in our closet."

"I know that, but then I left it alone. I thought we'd both left it alone until that night you gave me some, and that's when I realized you'd never stopped. You lied to me Denise, so both of us are at fault."

Denise stabbed Derrek in his forehead with her finger. "No, *you're* the one at fault. You're the one who started this cocaine thing, started using crack—yeah, I know all about that—and then gambled all our daughter's money away. This is all your fault, Derrek, and I'll never forgive you for it."

"Oh, so, what you're telling me is that you're done using drugs? That if I searched through this room, I wouldn't find a single Vicodin, bag of cocaine, or anything? Is that what you're sayin'?"

"I don't have to explain anything to you, and I want you out of here." Denise snatched the alarm clock from the nightstand and tossed it at him. "Get out!" she screamed, now hurling a picture frame at him.

"Mom! Dad!" Mackenzie shrieked, rushing into the room. "Please don't fight. Please," she begged, weeping loudly.

Denise stopped in her tracks and set Derrek's wooden watch box back on the dresser. She'd been planning to fling that at him, too, along with anything else she could find, if that's what it would take to make him leave. She wanted him gone, and she meant it.

"Honey, I'm sorry we woke you," Denise said. "I'm sorry you had to witness any of this."

"But it's okay. Daddy did a terrible thing, but all that matters is that you love each other and we're still a family."

Clearly, Mackenzie had heard their entire argument, and Denise hated that. She hated this whole fiasco.

"Mom, please," Mackenzie said, hugging her. "Please don't make Daddy leave. Please let's just forget about all this."

Denise held her daughter closely. "Honey, your dad and I are having a lot of problems right now, but I promise you everything is going to be fine. And no matter what happens, we'll never stop loving you."

"I know that, Mom, but I don't want you to stop loving each other, either. I want you to stop doing all those drugs, so things can be normal again."

Derrek looked at Denise, but she rolled her eyes at him. "Sweetie, I want you to go back to your room, okay?"

"But, Mom—"

"Honey, please. Just go to your room, and I'll come see you in a few minutes."

Mackenzie gazed at her mom and dad, her face soaked with tears, and left.

Denise closed the door and folded her arms. "You know what, Derrek? I'm not sure I can stay married to you after all this, but the very least you could do is replace Mackenzie's money. You can take it from your retirement account."

"No, Denise, actually I can't."

"Why?"

"It's gone."

Denise's heart pounded. "Gone where?"

"I gambled it all away at the casino. It's been gone for months."

Chapter 23

Another day had passed, yet here Denise was strolling back and forth through the bedroom still not speaking to Derrek. He knew he'd made a ton of terrible mistakes, but why couldn't she see that he was human and that this was what humans did? No one was perfect, everyone fell short every now and then, so why did she expect him to be any different? Why couldn't she just love him and forgive him the way God expected a wife to do? Had it been Denise who had gambled all their money away, sure he would have been upset and disappointed, but eventually he would have forgiven her and moved on. His first thought was that maybe all Denise needed was a little more time to accept what had happened, but it was the look in her eyes that told him otherwise. The way she gawked at him would have been considered frightening by most people's standards, and she acted as though she were repulsed by him. She acted as though they barely knew each other and more like they were opponents in a wrestling match.

Derrek watched as she passed by the chaise he was sitting on and wondered what he could say to make her talk to him. He certainly didn't want to bring up anything relating to money because now that he'd met D.C. at the credit union yesterday morning and cleaned out what was left of Mackenzie's college fund, he knew Denise was more furious than before. Then, if that hadn't been enough, he'd broken the news about his 401(k) plan to her. He just couldn't understand what had come over him a few months ago, but what he did know was that it had taken only one visit to the casino and he was hooked. He'd always stayed away from places like that but then one evening after work, Warren had encouraged him to tag along with him and a couple of other guys, and Derrek had agreed. He'd loved the adrenaline rush, along with the excitement of winning—which he now knew had been nothing more than beginner's luck—but from that day on, he'd looked forward to sneaking out to the casino every chance he'd gotten. He'd gone as much as he could with Warren, but then it hadn't been long before he'd begun missing a day here and a day there from work, so he could slip off and play a few slot machines. He hadn't realized he had a problem until he'd received a pension statement, showing that his retirement savings balance was zero and that he'd now have to pay it all back through a rather large monthly payroll deduction. Denise handled the finances in their house, but for whatever reason, she'd never paid close attention to his retirement fund. He guessed because she'd assumed it wasn't necessary.

Denise slipped on the blazer to her pantsuit and reached for her briefcase.

Derrek locked his fingers together. "Baby, how long are you going to keep this up? You haven't said one word to me since yesterday morning, and now today it's no different."

Denise searched through her handbag but never looked his way.

"Baby, I know I was wrong, and I know it's gonna take a lot of work to get us out of this mess we're in, but we can do it. We can do it together."

Denise closed her handbag and started for the doorway.

Derrek left the chaise and stood in front of it.

Denise frowned. "Will you please get out of my way? I know *you* have all the time in the world to sit here talking about nothing, but I have a job to get to."

"I know that, baby, but I really need to talk to you. I want you to know how sorry I am, and how I never meant to hurt you or Mackenzie. And, baby...I'm through doing drugs."

"You must think I'm a fool. You were out past eleven o'clock last night, yet you're standing here claiming you don't do drugs anymore? Derrek, please."

"Baby, I won't even lie to you. Warren and another friend of ours smoked up the rest of what I bought from Butch, but when I left there I promised myself that was the end. I thought long and hard about Mackenzie and my responsibility to her as a father, and I'm finished."

"Yeah, whatever. Now, will you please move so I can go?"

"Not until you talk to me."

"About what?" She frowned.

"Us working things out. And how it's time you gave up drugs, too. It's time we both start going back to those NA meetings."

"Over my dead body. I'm never going back to that place again, so you can just forget that."

"So I guess you don't care about our daughter and her plea for us to stop what we're doing? You're just gonna keep poppin' prescription drugs and snortin' cocaine no matter what."

"I can stop on my own, and that's what I'm gonna do."

"When?"

"When I'm good and ready. And anyway, as you can see, I'm not like you. I didn't lose my job, I didn't gamble away thousands of dollars, and I certainly didn't steal from my own child. Not to mention, I'm not the product of two low-life junkies."

Denise's words slashed his heart in two. He'd never heard her speak so maliciously to anyone, and he was very hurt by it. She was consumed with fury, and if he hadn't known better, he would have sworn she wanted to inflict bodily harm on him. He was also glad Mackenzie had ridden to school with Alexis this morning, because he would never want her to overhear any of this.

"Gosh," he finally replied. "I can't believe you said that."

"Oh yeah? And I can't believe you turned out to be such a loser. All these years, I thought I knew you, but now I realize I never did. So much for the *perfect* marriage I thought we had."

Derrek walked away from her, mumbling. "Hmmph, that's part of the reason we're having these problems."

"What did you say?"

"Nothing."

"No, tell me."

"Just leave it alone, Denise."

"Oh, so now I'm Denise again, huh? Why don't you man up and just say what you have to say."

"Okay, I will. This whole perfect marriage–perfect life thing is part of the reason we both started using in the first place."

Denise dropped her briefcase and purse onto the bed. "And how is that, Derrek?"

"You know exactly what I mean. This great desire you've always had to please your father and do whatever he expects. Everything is about appearances with him, so the two of us have always had to act like a couple of robots."

Denise laughed out loud. "Don't you *dare* blame my father for your mistakes. You're the one who made all those stupid choices."

"Yeah, but maybe if I'd felt a little more comfortable about seeing a psychologist—and I'm talking years ago—I never would have started doing drugs. I knew I had all these issues from childhood I was dealing with, but you were more worried about what people would think if they found out I was in counseling. You said that as long as we loved each other, I would be fine, so I left the whole idea of it alone."

"Wow, so you're gonna use some long-lost conversation from more than ten years ago? You're using that as a way to excuse your actions?"

"No. All I'm trying to say is that you and I are both using drugs because of some very deep-rooted childhood issues. I've got issues, and so do you."

"Speak for yourself, because I'm fine."

"Really? So you're okay with the fact that when you were seven, you walked in on your father and two of your mother's cousins? Yet to this day, you've never even told her about it. At every family gathering, those women smile in your mom's face, knowing good and well they slept with her husband. Let alone how pathetic it is that your father would even consider sleeping with two women at the same time and in the same bed he shared with his wife."

Denise grabbed her briefcase again. "I don't wanna talk about this."

"Well, I do," Derrek said, walking over and blocking the door. "And I guess you're also okay with the fact that you were eighteen before you *accidentally* found out you were adopted? And even then, your father did everything he could to try to cover it up."

Denise's eyes watered. "Why are you doing this?"

"Because, baby, it's time you dealt with all your skeletons. It's time you stopped pretending that you had the perfect childhood and that our lives just couldn't be better. We're both very messed up, and we have to do something. We have to fix *us* before we can fix anything else."

"No, Derrek, *you're* messed up because your parents have been strung out for years, and you don't have a relationship with them. But it's like I just told you, I'm fine."

"You're fine, huh?"

"Yes." Denise spoke with solid conviction.

"So I guess it doesn't matter that you used to cry yourself to sleep whenever your father came home drunk and beat your mother. And you and I both know he's likely *still* doing it. Your uppity, high-class father who's a partner at one of the most prestigious law firms in Chicago. And none of that matters to you?"

"Why are you using things I shared with you in confidence? Why are you using my personal business against me?"

"I'm just trying to get you to see that hiding all these family secrets and pretending that they didn't happen isn't good."

Denise shook her head in disbelief, backed away from him, grabbed her purse, and rushed toward the bathroom. Derrek ran behind her. As she stepped into the room where the toilet was, she attempted to shut the door, but Derrek barricaded it with his foot.

"Baby, no! You're not doing drugs today."

"Derrek, please leave me alone!"

Derrek struggled to pull her purse away from her. "No, I said you're not doing this."

Denise flung her arms wildly, striking him across his face and chest.

"Baby, I said no." Derrek jerked the purse completely out of her hand and the contents scattered across the floor.

As soon as Denise spotted her bag of cocaine she dived toward it, but Derrek hit the floor next to her and snatched it up.

Denise grabbed hold of it, both of them panting and tussling back and forth, trying to take control. Finally, Derrek jerked it as hard as he could, got up and went back to the toilet, poured out every speck of cocaine, and flushed it.

"Are you crazy?" Denise screamed.

"Baby, you need help. We both do."

"I hate you! I hate that I ever married you."

Derrek tried to slow his breathing and heard the phone ringing. With all the commotion, he wasn't sure if he should answer it or not, but he went to see who was calling. He frowned when he saw the name of Mackenzie's school displayed on the Caller ID screen.

"Hello?"

"Mr. Shaw?" a woman said in a panic. "This is Mrs. Donaldson, the school principal."

"Yes."

"Mackenzie passed out in the hallway and an ambulance is rushing her to the hospital. So, you need to get over there as fast as you can."

"Was she conscious before she left?"

"No...she wasn't. And they're taking her to Covington Memorial. I know you work there, and it's also the closest hospital to our school."

"Thank you so much for calling. We're on our way."

Derrek dropped the phone on the bed—the same phone he'd spoken to Dixon on the night he had died—and a sub-zero chill swept through him.

"Dear Lord, please, don't let this be happening again. Please don't take my daughter."

Chapter 24

$\mathcal{D}$enise, Derrek, and Wilma sat in the conference room they'd been escorted into and waited for the doctor to come in. Denise had called her mom while she and Derrek were en route.

"What's taking them so long?" Denise said, standing up and pacing back and forth. "Why won't they come tell us what's going on?" She hugged herself and wondered why she felt so restless. It was as if she couldn't sit still, and she could kill Derrek for flushing her coke down the toilet. He'd had no right, and it wasn't like she'd been planning to do any more than a line or two, anyway, so she hadn't seen what the big deal was.

"Honey, why don't you sit down?" Wilma told her. "I know this is a tough time, but why don't you try to relax."

"I can't, Mom! I need to know what's wrong with my baby."

Wilma raised her eyebrows. "Honey, I was only trying to help. I'm sorry."

Denise sighed. "No, Mom, I'm the one who's sorry. I didn't mean to yell at you."

"I know you're worried. I am, too, so there's no need to apologize."

Denise glanced over at Derrek, and while she hadn't noticed it before, he looked as though he'd aged twenty years. His face was consumed with sadness, and he hadn't said a word since they'd walked in there.

"Why won't somebody please come tell us something?" Denise ranted, walking over to the door and opening it. She looked up and down the hallway, but didn't see any doctors heading their way. "Geez."

Denise closed the door, sat down in her chair and stood back up again. She just couldn't be still, and now she caught Derrek gawking at her. "What?"

Derrek shook his head and kept staring at her, but he still wouldn't say anything. Denise could tell her mother felt uncomfortable and had sensed a while ago that something wasn't quite right between her daughter and son-in-law. She smiled, though, and pretended nothing was wrong.

"I'm sure Mackenzie is going to be fine," Wilma said. "You know that granddaughter of mine. Always on the go and involved in every kind of school activity there is. So knowing her she passed out from exhaustion."

"I hope you're right, Mom. I hope it's nothing serious."

Another ten minutes passed and the attending physician finally walked in. He was a handsome man, maybe in his early fifties.

"I'm very sorry to have kept you waiting, but we've had a time trying to get that little young lady of yours stabilized. It's good to see you, Derrek," he said, shaking his hand, "and I'm sorry it's not under better circumstances. I assume this is your wife."

"Yes, this is Denise, and my mother-in-law, Wilma."

"I'm Dr. Lancaster," he said. "Well, there's no easy way to say this, so I'll just come right out with it: Your daughter took a lot of pills, and she overdosed. We're doing a tox screen, of course, but since we found what looked to be one Vicodin left in an unlabeled bottle, we believe that's the culprit."

Denise sucked in her breath. "You must be mistaken."

"No, we had to pump her stomach, and the only reason we knew to do that was because the paramedics searched through her backpack and found this." Dr. Lancaster passed a folded piece of paper over to Derrek. "And just so you know, only the paramedics, one of the ER nurses, and myself have seen this, so I'm hoping you'll just be able to deal with this privately. I've known you for a long time, Derrek, so we'll try to keep this as quiet as possible."

Denise frowned and moved closer to her husband. "What does it say?"

Derrek read it, passed it on to Denise, and covered his face.

Dear Mom and Dad,

I've prayed and asked God not to let me die, but if I do, all I want is for both of you to stop using drugs forever. I want you to stop before you end up hating each other even more than you already do or you both end up killing yourselves. Also, please don't think I'm crazy because the only reason I did this was so that both of you could see just how dangerous drugs really are. I wanted you to see exactly what they can do to you if you keep using them. Mom, you take Vicodin and snort cocaine every single day, and Daddy, yesterday I heard Mom say you were now smoking crack. Also, Daddy, drugs are the reason you no longer have a job, and Mom has no idea how we're going to make it. She says we're going to be fine, but Mom says that about everything. I'm old enough to know, though, that if there's only one paycheck coming in and there's no savings left in the bank, we're going to be kicked out of our house and we'll have no place to go. We'll have no choice but to live on the street because Grandpa will never let us move in with them. Not once he finds out about the drugs. He'll see us as a huge disgrace, and he'll cut us off for good. We'll never see him or Granny ever again.

So please, please, I'm begging you both to go get some help. I want so badly to ask you to do it for me, but I saw online where all the support group sites say that if a person is addicted to drugs, they have to do it for themselves. They have to take the first step.

I'm very sorry that I did what I did, but when I heard both of you arguing yesterday and then, Mom, when I heard you say you wanted Daddy to move out, I knew I had to do something. I had to do whatever I could to make you stop using drugs before it was too late.

I love you both with all my heart, and I hope you can forgive me.

Mac

"Sweetie," Wilma said. "What does it say? And what little thug forced her to take those pills?"

Denise folded the letter back up and gazed at Dr. Lancaster. She fell back in her chair while tears streamed down her face. She was in a daze. "I . . . really don't know what to say. I mean, I can't believe our daughter would do something like this. She's such a smart girl, and this is so unlike her."

Dr. Lancaster didn't say anything.

Derrek turned to her. "But you know everything she said in that letter is true. Everything, Denise. And this whole drug madness was too much for her. We pushed her over the edge, and it's all our fault."

Denise stood up. "Oh dear God, what have we done? What have we done to our little girl?"

Derrek sniffled a couple of times and wiped his face. "So what now, Doctor? Is she going to be okay?"

"Well, as I said we did get her stabilized, but her nervous

system was suppressed and she stopped breathing. Actually, the paramedics had to revive her on the way here, so we're now breathing for her. We had to intubate her, and we're also waiting to see how high her liver enzymes are. The thing with Vicodin is that you're dealing with two totally different components. On the one hand, you have hydrocodone, which is an opiate, hence the reason she had breathing problems, and then there's the acetaminophen component which can cause liver failure."

Denise had been afraid of this because she knew breathing problems and liver issues were the top two symptoms of a Vicodin overdose. "Do you think she lost too much oxygen?"

"We're not sure. Once we do more tests, we'll have a better idea of what's going on with her brain function. And of course, the hope is that she'll wake up very soon."

Denise opened her mouth to ask another question, but there was a knock at the door.

Dr. Lancaster turned around. "Yes?"

As the door opened, Denise saw her father.

"I got here as fast as I could," he said, wearing one of his usual fifteen-hundred-dollar suits. Although, it might have cost more since he'd been known to spend as much as two thousand, depending on what mood he was in.

"Dr. Lancaster," Denise said. "This is my father, Charles."

"Nice to meet you." Charles took a seat next to his wife. "So is my granddaughter okay?"

Dr. Lancaster stood up. "If you don't mind, I'll let everyone else fill you in, so I can get back to my patient. But I'll keep you updated as often as I can."

"Thank you, Doctor," Derrek said.

Everyone else thanked him, too, and he left.

"So what's going on?" Charles asked.

Denise didn't know how to tell him, and she could tell her mother wasn't about to say a word. But Derrek spoke up right away.

"She OD'd on Vicodin."

Charles lowered his eyebrows. "She what? How?"

"She took a load of pills and passed out."

"But why would she do that?"

"Because your daughter and I have been addicted to drugs for more than a year now, I lost my job three days ago, and we don't have a dime to our names."

Denise closed her eyes. How could Derrek do this to her? How could he tell her father everything, not to mention all at once? He knew what kind of man he was dealing with, so why would he try to make trouble for them?

Charles cracked up laughing. "What is this, Denise, some kind of sick joke?"

Denise opened her eyes, wanting to call Derrek a liar, but she knew they were beyond that. She knew for Mackenzie's sake as well as her and Derrek's it was time she told her father the truth—that his daughter, son-in-law, and granddaughter weren't as perfect as he'd demanded them to be.

"No, Daddy, it's not. Everything Derrek told you is the truth, and I'm sorry you had to find out this way." Denise grabbed her mother's hand. "And I'm sorry you had to find out this way, too, Mom."

"I knew you shouldn't have married this fool," Charles shouted, standing up and shoving his chair away from the table. "He's the one who turned you on to this crap, isn't he? I always knew he was bad news. I knew just as soon as I found out his parents were crackheads, and I tried to tell you that."

"Daddy, please don't." Denise had never told Derrek about her father's objection to her marrying him, because she hadn't wanted to hurt his feelings. And then once she and her mother had convinced her father that Derrek was a good man with a good heart—a man who was well educated and who only wanted the best things in life—her father had changed his mind and given his blessings to Denise anyway.

"Wow, so now the truth comes out," Derrek said. "Now, all the family secrets have spilled out in the open . . . well maybe not all of them."

Denise grabbed Derrek's arm. "Oh God, Derrek please don't."

Derrek jerked away from her. "No, since your father thinks I'm such a loser and that I've never been good enough for you, I think your mom has a right to know."

Charles pursed his lips in disgust. "A right to know what?"

"That when Denise was seven she caught you gettin' your freak on with Liz and Betty. She caught you with two women at the same time . . . in the same bed you and your wife slept in every night. Now how pathetic is that? You're a woman beater *and* you slept with not one but two of your wife's cousins."

"That's a lie," Charles spat.

Derrek locked eyes with him. "I don't think so."

"Tell your mother the truth, Denise! Tell her your idiot husband is lying."

Denise felt restless and agitated again, and all she wanted to do was run out of there. She would do anything to get away from Derrek, her father, and her mother—especially, since her mother sat there emotionless and obviously humiliated.

"Denise!" her father yelled. "Did you hear me?"

Denise glanced at Derrek, and for some reason she thought back to everything he'd said to her earlier. She hadn't wanted to admit it until now, but she knew he'd been right about all the secrets, the unrealistic expectations her father had forced on all of them, and how her horrible childhood had played a major role in where they'd ended up today. So she inhaled and exhaled deeply. "No, Mom, Derrek isn't lying, and I'm sorry."

Wilma swallowed and looked straight ahead, acting as though her daughter hadn't told her a thing. Denise knew her mother would never acknowledge the truth, but at least Denise had owned up to what she'd seen, and it was a relief to finally free her own conscience. Until now, she'd never fully realized how much that dreadful incident with her father had scarred her emotionally.

Charles squinted his eyes at his daughter. "So now this fool has you lying for him I guess. Wilma, let's go."

Denise's mother finally spoke up. "But, honey, what about Mackenzie? She's not out of the woods yet, and I don't want to leave her. Honey, please, don't make me leave our grand-daughter."

"Fine. You stay here, but I'm leaving."

Denise gazed at her father with pleading eyes. "Daddy, I'm sorry, but it's time we stop hiding things. It's time we face the truth."

Charles scowled at his daughter, flung the chair he'd been sitting in across the room, and stormed out.

Denise sat in silence, but she knew her relationship with her father had changed forever.

Chapter 25

$\mathcal{H}$ours had passed, and while Mackenzie had moved from the ER to the intensive care unit, there hadn't been much change. The toxicology report had confirmed what they already knew, that it had been Vicodin that Mackenzie had taken, but she was still unconscious. Denise had prayed harder than ever before, and she just wished her baby would wake up. She wished there would be some sign of improvement, some sign of hope.

Denise looked at her best friend, Michelle, who was sitting on the other side of Wilma, and smiled. Michelle was such a great friend, and Denise felt awful about the way she'd treated her for so many months now. She hadn't wanted to keep her distance, but now she realized the reason she'd done so was because she hadn't wanted to take the chance on having Michelle find out her secret. She hadn't wanted her to know that cocaine had become a permanent staple in her and Derrek's lives. She hadn't thought about it much before today, but now she knew she was deeply ashamed of what they'd been doing and she hadn't wanted anyone outside of their household to know about it. Doing things that weren't morally right and then hiding them and pretending they'd never happened was the way she'd been taught to handle things. Her father had trained her well, and now she was paying a very steep price for it. She would never try to deny the fact that she was a grown woman who'd made her own choices, but she just wished she'd been raised with better examples. She wished her parents had been a lot more transparent and a lot less secretive because pretending to be something you weren't was never good for anyone. If anything, it was detrimental to the soul. To put it plainly, whenever a person did this, all it meant was that they were living a lie.

Denise leaned her head against the wall and turned toward Derrek, who was sitting next to her, but she didn't say anything. She could tell he didn't feel well, and she knew it was for the same reason she felt pretty badly herself. Earlier in the day, she'd been restless, but now she felt exhausted and like she had flu symptoms. There was no doubt she was suffering from malaise, which was one of many cocaine withdrawal symptoms. She and Derrek had both come way down from the highs they'd been on the night before, and Denise wondered if Derrek was craving coke as badly as she was. She didn't know about him, but for her, the craving aspect was the worst symptom of all because with the exception of her wanting Mackenzie to get well physically and emotionally, there was nothing else she wanted more right now than to snort a couple of lines of cocaine. But she knew for the sake of her daughter and their family, she had to forego it. She had to stay clean and get the kind of help Mackenzie had insisted they needed.

Denise did understand her daughter's plea, and she knew she was right. But what she still couldn't fully wrap her brain around was the idea that Mackenzie had taken pills from her bathroom drawer and swallowed enough to overdose. She'd done it on purpose and while she was at school. Had she truly believed this was the only way she could get her and Derrek's attention? Had they actually pushed her to such major extremes? Denise asked herself those questions, but she knew the answer was a resounding yes across the board.

Then, there was her poor mother, who sat on the other side of her, acting as though the subject of her husband having an affair with her two cousins hadn't come up. It was as if she hadn't heard Derrek. Or maybe she was trying to convince herself that none of what he'd disclosed was true, but either way, she seemed unmoved. Denise knew she *had* heard every single word, though, and her mother also knew Denise would never lie about her father.

Michelle slightly leaned forward. "Denise, are you sure I can't get you guys anything? Something to eat? Something to drink?"

"You know," Denise said. "Actually, I think I'll have some coffee."

"Derrek?" Michelle said.

Surprisingly, he responded. "If you don't mind, I'll take a cup, too."

"Cream and sugar?"

"Yes," he said.

"Same for me," Denise added.

Wilma grabbed both handles of her Louis Vuitton satchel. "I think I'll walk down with you. Need to stretch my legs a little."

Denise stood up and hugged Michelle. "Thank you so much for being here. Especially, since I really haven't been much of a friend lately."

"Girl, please. Don't say another word, and I'll be here for as long as you need me."

Denise watched as Michelle and Wilma strolled out of the waiting room and knew she'd eventually have to sit Michelle down and tell her everything. As her best friend, she owed her at least that much.

After about two minutes, Denise got up and moped through

the waiting room. But when she turned and looked back at Der-rek, his eyes were closed. So she stepped out into the hallway, spoke to a few folks passing by, and then walked back into the waiting room. Gosh, if only she could get her hands on a little coke. All she needed was just a tiny bit to get her through the rest of the afternoon and possibly through the evening. That's all. After that, she would be through for good. She tried to think of other options, but unfortunately, there weren't any and she just couldn't help herself. What she needed to do was call Butch so he could bring her a small bag just as soon as possible. Plus, she needed to pay him the two hundred dollars she owed him from Wednesday, anyway, which she could easily do now since it was Friday and her paycheck had been deposited. Actually, both her and Derrek's checks were in their account. She knew this because as soon as she'd awakened this morning, she'd gone down to the study and checked on the computer. Just as she'd figured three days ago, they barely had enough to cover all the bills that were due, but she needed to use some of the money to get her head right. She needed something to lift her up, so she could be there for her daughter.

But as Denise walked closer to the elevator, preparing to head down to the first floor to phone Butch in private, the words "code blue" roared across the PA system. She knew all too well what code blue meant, so she stopped in her tracks and prayed it wasn't for Mackenzie. She prayed her daughter hadn't turned for the worse. But when the automatic doors flung open, and a visitor exited the intensive care unit, Denise heard a woman yelling, "Hurry, it's the thirteen-year-old. She's gone into cardiac arrest."

Chapter 26

Now, that the news had been confirmed, there wasn't a dry eye in the room. Derrek held Denise as closely as he possibly could, both of them shedding a river of tears, and Michelle and Wilma wiped their faces to no avail. Even little Alexis, Mackenzie's friend, and her parents, each of whom had just arrived a few minutes ago, were devastated. Everyone sat in total disbelief, and Derrek wondered if his daughter was going to make it. He'd already known she was in bad shape, just from the report Dr. Lancaster had given them earlier in the day, but now things had gotten worse. As of a half hour ago, Mackenzie had slipped further and further toward a life-or-death situation, and Derrek knew there was a great chance they would lose her.

Derrek stroked the back of his wife's hair and tried to gain his composure; partly for his own sense of sanity and partly so Denise wouldn't lose it completely.

Michelle stood up and patted tears from the corner of her eyes. "Denise and Derrek? If you don't mind, I'd like to say a prayer for Mackenzie."

Wilma rose to her feet. "I think that would be wonderful." Then she reached over and caressed Denise's back. "Honey, why don't you try to stand up?"

It took a while, but Denise finally allowed Derrek to help her up from her chair. Now, all of them stood in a circle with their eyes shut, holding hands.

"Dear heavenly Father, we come right now thanking You for keeping Mackenzie in Your loving care. We thank You for watching over her, Father, and we ask that You would totally heal her mind and body. We know that You are a miracle worker and that no illness is too great for You, so we humbly ask that You bring her back to perfect health. We also ask that You would please bless this entire family. Give them comfort, Lord, and please give them the strength they need to endure this very difficult time in their lives. Father God, we ask these and all Your many wonderful blessings in Your Son Jesus's name. Amen."

The room was quiet for a few seconds, but suddenly, Denise wailed loudly, broke away from Derrek's embrace, grabbed her purse and tore out of the family consultation room. Derrek ran behind her.

"Denise, wait!" he yelled, but she kept running so Derrek moved faster. Soon, she arrived at the elevator, and that's when he caught up to her. "Baby, where are you going?"

"I have to get out of here."

"To go where?"

"I just need some air."

The elevator doors opened, a family of four stepped off, and Denise and Derrek got on. Denise pushed the button for the main floor, and while Derrek didn't know what else to say to her, he wasn't about to let her leave the hospital.

When the doors opened again, she hurried into the hallway, heading toward the exit to the parking lot. Derrek stayed close to her, and when they both pushed through the turnstile and down the side of the building, he grabbed her arm.

"Baby, what is it?"

Denise finally stopped. "Derrek, you have no idea what I was planning to do before I heard that code called."

"What are you talking about?"

"I'm so ashamed, but I couldn't help myself. One thought led to another and the next thing I knew, I was..."

"You were what?"

"About to call Butch. Baby, I was actually going to call and ask him to bring me some coke. Here at the hospital where our daughter is fighting for her life. Can you believe that?"

Derrek put his hands in his pockets. "Yeah... unfortunately, I do. I believe you because for hours now, it has taken everything in me not to call Butch myself. I've been struggling the whole time, and that's why I haven't said very much. I thought it was best just to keep quiet and try to deal with it, but it's not working."

"The only thing that stopped me from calling him was Mackenzie. But if I hadn't heard the words 'code blue,' I'm not sure what would have happened."

Derrek grabbed Denise's hand and sighed. "You know... I've been doing a lot of thinking. We've got a serious problem, and if we don't do something now, we're not gonna make it. And after the way I've felt today, I now know that meetings won't be enough. What you and I need is in-patient rehab."

Denise looked away from him.

Derrek waited a couple of seconds and gently turned her face back toward him. "Baby, are you with me?"

Denise gazed into his eyes, but he couldn't tell what she was thinking.

"Baby, you know we have to do this. There's no other way."

Denise still didn't say anything.

"I realize the thought of rehab is a very scary thing, but with God's help, I think we'll be fine. To be honest, you and I have never really depended on God enough. This morning, I thought a lot about my grandparents and everything they taught me, and that's when I realized how wrong I've been about my parents. They were wrong, too, but I still should have done everything I could to help them. I've made so many mistakes when it comes to my family, including the way I treated Dixon. But if it's the last thing I do, I'm going to try my best to make up for it. I'm going to do exactly what Dixon asked me to do at the end of that letter he wrote me. He wanted me to forgive our parents and do whatever I could for them. So, baby, I'm asking you . . . please."

Denise stared at him a few seconds longer and then said, "Okay, yes, I'll go. I'll go to rehab, but when?"

"Now."

"But what about Mac? We can't just leave her. Not when she's had a life-threatening setback."

"I know. I've already thought about that. But, baby, we're no good to her like this. We can't help *her* until we help ourselves."

Denise folded her arms against her chest. "I don't know about this."

"It'll be hard leaving her, but it's for the best. Plus, as much as I hate thinking about it, this is what Mac wants. She placed her own life in danger, trying to save us."

Denise hugged him with tears falling again. She did this for what seemed an eternity, but finally, she surrendered. "Okay, I'll do it. I'll do whatever it takes to get well."

Chapter 27

*I*t was tremendously hard watching her little girl lying in bed unconscious, and Denise could barely stand it. After making their decision to enter a treatment facility, Denise and Derrek had come straight back up to the intensive care unit, and one of the nurses had told them they could look in on Mackenzie. She had finally been stabilized, but with all the attachments, including an IV in her arm, a breathing tube down her throat, and a monitor recording her blood pressure and heart rate, it was still hard to be hopeful. During Denise's time working as a nurse at this very hospital, she'd certainly seen much worse, but somehow it was different seeing her own daughter in this situation.

Denise moved closer to the bed, and Derrek placed his arm around her waist. At least she seemed comfortable and not in any pain.

Denise reached over the bed railing and held her hand. "Sweetie, it's Mom. We're here, baby."

"We're both here," Derrek said, "and we love you very much."

Denise shut her eyes tightly and took a deep breath, doing all she could not to cry. "Honey, your dad and I are so sorry for everything we've done. We're sorry for all the pain we caused you, and we're finally going to get the help we need. We're going to do what we should have done a long time ago, just like you wanted."

Derrek rubbed his daughter's leg through the blanket.

"While we're gone, though," Denise said, "your granny, Michelle, and Alexis's mom are going be here watching out for you. One of them will be here every single day, and knowing your granny, she'll be spending the night even."

"You're also in one of the best hospitals in the area," Derrek added, "so we know you'll be well taken care of."

Denise and Derrek turned around when they heard Mackenzie's door opening. It was Dr. Lancaster.

He patted Derrek on the shoulder. "So, you both hangin' in there?" he asked.

"As much as we can," Derrek said. "And we've also decided to enter a twenty-eight-day program. We know this isn't the best time, but..."

"I understand, but not only have you made a very brave choice, you've made the right one. And of course, we're going to do all we can for Mackenzie. That I can assure you of."

Denise and Derrek smiled and thanked Dr. Lancaster, but when Denise turned back to their daughter, she thought she'd seen her head moving. She waited a few seconds, though, and sure enough, it happened again. Mackenzie moved her head a couple more times and slowly opened her eyes. She blinked quite a bit and soon scanned the room.

Denise covered her mouth with her hands. "Oh, dear Lord, thank You, thank You, thank You!"

Derrek was filled with joy, as well. "Thank You, Lord, for answering our prayers."

It was obvious that Mackenzie was still a little out of it because of how heavily sedated she was, but Denise wasn't planning to leave there without making sure she could hear them.

"Sweetie, if you can understand me, squeeze my hand."

Mackenzie did as she was asked, and Denise's heart raced. She knew Mackenzie still had a long way to go before she'd be considered well, but Denise was just happy she could communicate on any level.

"I have something to ask you, and if your answer is yes, I want you to squeeze my hand. Can you do that?"

Mackenzie squeezed her mother's hand again.

"Your dad and I are going away to get some help. So, is that okay with you?"

Mackenzie squeezed Denise's hand, but this time she held it much tighter than she had the first time. Their daughter had so much strength and wisdom to only be thirteen, and while Denise had sort of still been struggling with the idea of leaving Mackenzie—even as much as only a few minutes ago—she now had no doubt they were doing the right thing, the same as Dr. Lancaster had told them. She'd also had a few reservations about being locked up for four solid weeks, but again, she now knew they'd made the right decision. They were taking responsibility for their actions and were willing to sacrifice whatever they had to, including money, material possessions, and social status. And while her father would likely never speak to her again because of it, she was proud of herself. She was proud of Derrek, and strangely enough, she felt better than she had in a long time.

And this, of course, was a good thing.

Epilogue

A Year Later

As Denise looked back at the last twelve months, it was hard to fathom all they'd been through. Thank God Mackenzie had fully recovered, but it had only been after a number of medical setbacks and counseling sessions that she'd started to feel like her old self again. She'd had lots of issues with her liver, but the good news was that even though she'd eventually lost 50 percent of it because of multiple surgeries, her liver was completely back intact. The liver was the only internal organ capable of natural regeneration, so Denise was grateful that Mackenzie had benefited from that reality.

Then there was her and Derrek and their recovery process. As planned, they'd gone into treatment, but per the advice of two different psychologists, they'd gone to separate facilities. This had made things a little harder for Denise, maybe more for her than it had for Derrek, but she'd still agreed to follow through. The withdrawal period had been the worst part of all due to the excessive cocaine cravings and physical sickness it had brought about, but Denise and Derrek had survived. Denise had also finally faced her demons: the void she'd always felt in her life after learning she'd been abandoned by her biological mother; seeing her father having the most perverted kind of sex she could think of with two women she was related to; and then the memories of her father getting sloppy drunk and beating her mother for no reason. Through therapy, she'd come to realize just how deeply she'd suppressed those thoughts and feelings, and she was glad to no longer be in denial about them.

Denise had also experienced another revelation the moment she'd seen Derrek again: she could never, ever love a man more than she loved him. This truth had become so apparent to her that it was hard for her to imagine how, when Derrek had lost his job and all their money, she'd hardly been able to stand him. She'd practically despised him and had wanted him to move out, but now she knew her ill feelings toward him had been fueled by addiction, and that she hadn't been thinking straight. Actually, neither she nor Derrek had been capable of doing anything in the manner they should have, and they'd suffered great consequences because of it. They'd lost their home and both their vehicles, and Denise's father hadn't spoken to either of them since that day he'd come to the hospital. On several different occasions, Denise had tried contacting him by phone, but he'd refused to take her calls. He'd also made it very clear through Denise's mother that while his granddaughter would always be welcome in *his* home, Denise and Derrek were to never set foot back there again. He'd told his wife that she could get out, too, if she didn't like it, but sadly, Denise knew her mother would never leave him. Her mother would willingly stay with her husband until death, regardless of how many terrible things he said or did to her. So, Denise was happy just being able to see her when she could, that is when her mother could sneak away for a visit.

But the blessing in all of this was that even though they'd lost everything, they still had each other and believe it or not, life was good again. When Denise had first gone into rehab, Mr. Hunter had told her how happy he was about it and that her job would be waiting for her when she was ready. However, when Denise had been released, she'd thanked Mr. Hunter and told him she didn't think returning to such a stressful job was good for her recovery, and that she was going to look for a home health care position; preferably one that allowed her to work at various assisted-living locations. There was no doubt that her love for working with older people hadn't changed, but her priorities in life had done a drastic one-eighty, and she was okay with that. It was true that she now earned only half the salary she had in previous years and so did Derrek, now that he worked as a branch manager at a bank, but they were still much happier and more at peace with who they were as human beings. They were free to be the kind of people they wanted to be, and they no longer had to put on airs—meaning they could live in the condo they now rented because they no longer had the kind of credit to buy one, they could drive basic cars that hadn't cost a ridiculous amount of money, and they could focus more on each other than they did on status and how to maintain it. They could also freely attend a very small Bible-based church where they were learning a lot and proudly attend Narcotics Anonymous meetings regularly. They could do all of this and more and not have to worry about what others thought of them.

Yes, life was good—not easy by any means—but still good, and as Denise looked at her daughter sitting across the table from them and then at her mother-in-law and father-in-law, she smiled and slipped her arm inside of Derrek's. Derrek had picked up his parents from the drug recovery shelter they'd been living at for two months, and the five of them were having dinner at Wendy's—versus dining at one of the more higher-priced restaurants Denise, Derrek, and Mackenzie had regularly eaten at in the past. Denise was proud of Derrek for the way he'd kept his word about helping his parents, and while his mother still seemed a bit on edge and like she was ready to break and run to the nearest drug house on a moment's notice, Derrek's father was working as hard as he could, trying to complete the year-long program they were participating in.

So, yes, there they sat at a popular fast-food restaurant as happy as could be, and it was because of this that something dawned on Denise. For years, she'd been sure that she and Derrek were the perfect couple with the perfect life, but now she knew different. Today, she realized that sometimes less really was more, and in their case, having less of everything had turned their lives around for the better. It had changed them in ways she'd never thought imaginable, and she was ecstatic about it.

This was by far the happiest she'd ever been in her life, and *this* incredible blessing alone was reason to be thankful, both now and—with much prayer, faith, and commitment—forever.

If you or a loved one is struggling with drug addiction, please visit the National Alcoholism and Substance Abuse Information Center at:

http://www.AddictionCareOptions.com.

You can also call the 24-hour
national hotline number at:

(800) 784-6776.

To find a Narcotics Anonymous meeting
in your area, please visit:

www.NA.org.

Discussion Questions for
The Perfect Marriage

1. At the beginning of the novel we see Denise and Derrek at a meeting for people who have problems with drug abuse. Considering the level of their drug use at the start of the story, do you think this meeting was necessary for them, or was it an overreaction? Why?

2. We often hear people refer to *social* smokers or *social* drinkers, meaning they only use nicotine or alcohol in a social atmosphere. Do you believe there is such a thing as a *social drug user*? What about prescription drugs? If a woman lends her friend a prescription pill to help her sleep or calm her nerves during an especially stressful event, is that drug abuse?

3. Denise and Derrek keep some pretty big secrets from one another, but it didn't start out that way. At first they only keep what they consider small secrets. Is it ever okay to keep a secret from your spouse? Or is keeping a secret of any kind harmful to a marriage?

4. We learn that Derrek and his brother, Dixon, had had a fight over money, and this is what had kept them apart. Do you think the issue was that Dixon didn't repay Derrek the money he borrowed, or that Derrek didn't approve of how Dixon spent the money? When a person gives another person a loan, do they have the right to judge how that money is spent?

5. Denise holds herself to very high standards—something she learned to do during her childhood. While the pressure she put on herself ultimately led to her problems, it also helped her to achieve a high level of success. How can someone balance striving to achieve her full potential and protecting herself from unrealistic expectations? As a parent, how can someone encourage her child to succeed without making her afraid to fail?

6. Both of Derrek's parents and his brother struggled with drug addiction. Do you think a propensity to become addicted to drugs is hereditary? If so, does that make Derrek's drug use more excusable (it was inevitable that he would use drugs) or does it make his behavior more irresponsible (knowing his family history he should have been more careful)?

7. When someone is struggling with addiction, what do we expect of the people around them? For example, should Denise's friend Michelle have noticed her odd behavior and questioned it more? Should Derrek's boss have spoken up sooner and encouraged him to get treatment rather than fire him? Or does the responsibility to change belong solely to the addict?

8. Denise and Derrek turn to drugs as a form of stress release. What are other, healthier ways they could have managed their stress?

9. Denise's mother, Wilma, is another character who keeps secrets from the people she loves. Why do you think Wilma keeps the truth about her marriage secret? Fear? Shame? Denial? How do you think her behavior impacted Denise?

10. Mackenzie was so desperate to save her family that she took dramatic—and dangerous—action. What might you have counseled her to do instead? And what advice would you offer her while she's healing, both physically and emotionally, from all she's been through?

11. It's not only drugs, alcohol, or gambling that people can become addicted to. People can develop addictions to food, shopping, the Internet—anything. Can an addiction ever be harmless? What advice would you give to someone battling an addiction?

12. Is there such a thing as a perfect marriage? What qualities must a marriage have to be described as perfect?

Will the newest addition to the Black family be the
blessing that brings them closer together—
or the final straw that will tear them apart?

Please turn this page
for an excerpt from

A House Divided.

Chapter 1

What a witch. For months, Vanessa Anderson, the *other* grand-mother, had been working Charlotte's last nerve, and Charlotte wished this heifer would vanish into thin air. Ever since hearing the news just over seven months ago about Matthew's girlfriend, Racquel, being pregnant, things had turned pretty ugly. At first, Vanessa had seemed like a decent enough woman, and her hus-band, Neil, a noticeably good man, but once Matthew had left for Harvard last fall, Vanessa's attitude had changed drastically. Now, though, it was the middle of January, and things had only gotten worse. Vanessa no longer answered Charlotte's phone calls or attempted to return them, and Racquel had suddenly begun answering a lot less, too. Racquel did talk to Charlotte every now and then, but mostly when Charlotte and Curtis received updates about Racquel's doctor visits, her ultrasound testing, and any other information relating to their grandchild, it came directly from Matthew. Of course, when Charlotte had asked Matthew why Vanessa was treating her like the enemy, Matthew had told her it was because Vanessa had begun feeling as though Char-lotte was trying to take over and control every decision relating to Racquel and the baby. Charlotte had been stunned, to say the least, because whether Vanessa liked it or not, Charlotte was going to be just as much a grandmother to Matthew and Racquel's baby as she was, and Charlotte had every right to ask as many questions and make as many suggestions as she wanted. This was going to be Charlotte and Curtis's very first grandchild, and she wouldn't back down for Vanessa, Racquel, or anyone else. It was the reason Charlotte was sitting front and center at this pathetic little baby shower, even though she knew Vanessa didn't want her there.

"Oh what a precious little christening outfit," one of Racquel's cousins said.

"It really is," a couple of other women commented. Other ladies cooed over the gorgeous little satin two-piece pant and jacket set, too.

Charlotte cast her eye at Vanessa, who was boiling, and then smiled at Racquel. "As soon as I saw it, I just had to buy it. It'll be perfect when Curtis christens the baby."

Vanessa set her coffee cup down on the small table next to her. "Hmmm. Well, I guess Racquel hasn't told you."

"Told me what?"

"That *our* pastor will be the one doing the christening. Pastor Collins has been our minister for more than twenty years, and he and his wife are Racquel's godparents."

Charlotte took a deep breath. She didn't want to show her behind in front of all these women, but if Vanessa didn't watch herself...

"No, actually," Charlotte said, "the subject has never come up. I just assumed that since Curtis is a pastor and since he's the baby's grandfather, this was a done deal."

Vanessa smirked at Charlotte. "Wow. Then, I guess it's a good thing we got this all cleared up. Now there won't be any misunderstandings."

It was all Charlotte could do not to fire back at Vanessa, but instead, she scanned the drab-looking family room they sat in. It was a shame they were bunched so close together. At least that's what it felt like to Charlotte, because had the shower taken place at her house, they'd have had a lot more room—not to mention the atmosphere would have been far more beautiful. Vanessa's decorating skills were average at best, and Charlotte was tempted to recommend a professional to her.

"Thank you so much for buying this, Mrs. Black," Racquel said nervously. Her tone was awkward, and Charlotte knew it was because Racquel was hoping this christening topic wouldn't spiral into a heated debate.

"You're quite welcome," Charlotte said. "I know we still don't know if you're having a boy or a girl, but I'm praying for a grandson, of course."

"Me, too," Racquel said, smiling and stroking her shoulder-length, thick brown mane to the side.

Charlotte wanted to ask her again why she didn't want to know the sex of the baby, because to her that was just ridiculous. Racquel had gotten Matthew to agree to that nonsense, too, and this had ruined Charlotte's plan of having a huge family get-together where everyone, including Matthew and Racquel, would find out the sex all at once. A couple of years ago, Charlotte had gone to a baby announcement party, where the ultrasound technician had written down the sex of the baby on a piece of paper, given it to the parents in a sealed envelope, and the parents had taken it to a bakery. The cake decorator had then told them that if they were going to have a girl, she'd make the inside of the cake pink, and if it was going to be a boy, she'd color it light blue. That way when they cut into it, it would be a surprise to everyone. Charlotte had loved that idea—but again, Racquel had spoiled everything. Charlotte's feelings toward Racquel had always been lukewarm at best, and this latest harebrained decision of hers hadn't helped. In fact, the only reason Charlotte tolerated her and stayed in contact with her was because she was carrying her precious little grandchild.

But Charlotte smiled as genuinely as she could. "Oh and hey...those other four boxes are from Curtis and me, too."

Racquel opened each of them, one by one. The contents included: an Elsa Peretti silver baby spoon from Tiffany, a silver frame for the baby's birth record, a five-hundred-dollar gift card from Target for disposable diapers or whatever else the baby needed, and another five hundred dollar gift card from Toys"R"Us.

"Thank you for everything," Racquel said. "This really was very kind of you and Pastor Black."

"Anything for our grandchild," Charlotte said, glaring at Vanessa. "Anything at all."

Racquel opened at least another twenty gifts that others had brought, and while not all of them would have been items Charlotte would have chosen for any baby, some of them were very thoughtful and in some instances very cute; especially some of the little onesies. Still, as Charlotte sat watching and trying her best to pretend as though she were happy to be there, she wished her mom or her best friend, Janine, had come with her. At least then, she wouldn't feel like some outcast and would have had someone familiar to talk to. But her mom and best friend not being there was all Vanessa's fault because, as it was, Charlotte hadn't found out about the shower herself until three days ago. Her mom had certainly wanted to attend, but since she was chairing a luncheon over in Chicago, she wouldn't be finished in time to make it. She and Charlotte's dad lived ninety minutes away, and as for Janine, she and her husband and daughter were away for the weekend in Wisconsin. Even now, Charlotte wanted to go off on Vanessa, because while Vanessa had claimed she'd mailed Charlotte's invitation two weeks ago along with all the others, Charlotte knew she was lying. Had it not been for Matthew asking her why she hadn't RSVPed, Charlotte never would have known about it, period. But that was okay, because even though Vanessa didn't want Charlotte in her home or anywhere near her, Charlotte was there, anyway, and she was planning to be around all the time as long as her grandchild was living here.

"So have you thought about names?" Laura asked. Laura, Racquel's great-aunt, was a classy, elegant woman with gorgeous white hair, but Charlotte could tell she was just as devious as Vanessa. It was clear, too, that she didn't care for Charlotte.

Racquel smiled. "Actually, Auntee Laura, we have. If it's a girl, her name will be Madison, and if it's a boy, Matthew Jr."

"You mean, Matthew the Second," Charlotte chimed in.

"No," Vanessa said, frowning. "She means Matthew Jr."

Charlotte stared at Vanessa. "I realize he'll be a Jr., but Matthew the Second sounds a lot more prestigious...and I'm sure we all want what's best for the baby. Especially when it comes to his getting into the right schools, colleges, and graduate programs, let alone when it's time for him to write a résumé."

Vanessa stood up. "You know what, Charlotte? We don't care about any of that nonsense. If my daughter says her son's name will be Matthew Jr., then that's exactly what it's going to be."

"Is that how you feel, too, Racquel?" Charlotte asked.

"Matt and I are both fine with Jr. We know how you feel, Mrs. Black, but Jr. is traditional, and that's what we've decided on."

"That's what you and my son have decided, or *you* and your *mother*?"

"Now, you wait just a minute," Vanessa said, stepping closer and pointing her finger in Charlotte's face. "Don't you ever speak to my daughter that way. And as a matter of fact, I want you outta here! We never wanted you to come in the first place."

Charlotte got to her feet and slapped Vanessa's finger away from her. "I knew all along you didn't want me to come, but I'm here, anyway. And for the record, you've got one more time to wave that decrepit-lookin' hand of yours in my face." Charlotte guessed Vanessa looked okay to be in her forties, which was about ten years older than she was, but Vanessa sure had a lot of wrinkles and she needed to do something about them.

"Mom...Mrs. Black," Racquel begged. "Please don't do this."

Vanessa stepped toe-to-toe with Charlotte. "And if you ever touch me again, you'll regret it for the rest of your life."

Laura rushed toward them. "Ladies, please. This isn't the time or place for this, and you're upsetting Racquel."

"Why can't you guys just get along?" Racquel asked in tears. "At least for the baby."

"Because this witch," Vanessa spat, "is out of line and is always trying to control everything. She thinks because she and her husband have a lot more money than we do that she should have a say-so in everything. But sweetheart," she said, turning back to Charlotte, "I've got news for ya. It ain't happenin'. My husband is a successful neurosurgeon, I have my own business, and we don't need you."

"Honey, whether you feel like you need me and my husband or not, you're stuck with us. That baby Racquel is carrying is just as much ours as it is yours—and if you push me, I'll be your worst nightmare."

Vanessa took her finger and jabbed it into Charlotte's shoulder. "Get out of my house! Get out or I'm calling the police."

Charlotte squinted and wrinkled her forehead. Then she pushed Vanessa. "You must be crazy, putting your hands on me."

Vanessa slapped Charlotte so hard the sound of it rang

throughout the family room. Charlotte smacked her back, and Vanessa grabbed the side of her face.

"You're going to jail!" Vanessa yelled.

No one moved or made a peep until Racquel stood up, grabbed her stomach, and screamed loudly. "Oh God, please don't do this!"

Racquel didn't look so well, and Charlotte hoped she was okay.

Vanessa wrapped her arm around her daughter. "Honey, why don't you sit back down."

But as soon as Racquel went to grab the arm of the chair, attempting to do just that, she grabbed her stomach and yelled at the top of her lungs. "Oh God, something's wrong," she said, doubling over. "Oh God, Mom...it hurts, it hurts, it hurts."

Vanessa helped her daughter over to the sofa, and Charlotte noticed how wet the inner parts of Racquel's pant legs were. Charlotte feared that her water had broken, and her heart skipped multiple beats.

"Oh no, Mom...dear God, please don't let me be losing my baby. Please, please, please," Racquel said, screaming.

"Someone call 911!" Vanessa said. "Now!"

Charlotte looked on, unable to move or say a word. She hoped this episode wasn't her and Vanessa's fault. If only Vanessa hadn't approached her the way she had, threatening her and trying to throw her out of their house. Charlotte prayed that Racquel and the baby were going to be fine, because she just couldn't lose her new grandchild. Not now. Not when he or she was so close to entering the world. Not when Charlotte had already lost a child of her own a few years ago. She simply couldn't bear the thought of going through that kind of pain again.

Worse, if something happened to Matthew's baby, and he found out that Charlotte and Vanessa may have been the cause, he would never forgive her. When Charlotte had had those two affairs on his dad two years ago, it had taken Matthew a long time to get over it, but with something like this, there would be no coming back from it. All the apologies and explanations in the world wouldn't be able to fix things, and Matthew would be done with her for good. He would likely disown her completely and never speak to her again.

Charlotte watched Racquel twist and turn on the sofa, moaning and crying, and her heart beat faster than before. *Oh God, please, please let Racquel and the baby be all right . . . especially the baby. I'm begging you.*